Ace walked to the
neither of them m

"Ace," Janet whispered fiercely under her breath, "don't you dare like that girl. Don't you dare be attracted to this woman."

"Why?" Ace whispered back.

"You know why," Janet said, looking at him meaningfully. "She could be Micky Wiley's daughter, and if she is, don't let me say it out loud…"

"What are you talking about, Aunt Janet?" Ace looked at Janet guiltily. He knew what she was implying, and for a moment, he didn't care.

"You know what I am talking about," Janet said below her breath. "Just in case you are still unclear about it. Micky Wiley was your mother's gardener. You look a little bit too much like Micky Wiley for anyone to be comfortable. Come to think of it, your mother was not very much unlike Charlotte in that regard."

"All of that is just rumor and conjecture." Ace whispered, he glanced at Kiya was watching him and his aunt furiously whispering a tentative smile on her face.

ACE

BRENDA BARRETT

JAMAICA
TREASURES

A CE

A Jamaica Treasures Book/January 2020
Published by Jamaica Treasures
Kingston, Jamaica

This is a work of fiction. Names, characters, places, and incidents are either the product of the author's imagination or are used fictitiously. Any resemblance to an actual person or persons, living or dead, events, or locales is entirely coincidental.

978-976-8247-73-5
Jamaica Treasures
P.O. Box 482
Kingston 19
Jamaica W.I.
www.fiwibooks.com

ALSO BY BRENDA BARRETT

FULL CIRCLE
NEW BEGINNINGS
THE PREACHER AND THE PROSTITUTE
AFTER THE END
THE EMPTY HAMMOCK
THE PULL OF FREEDOM
REBOUND SERIES
THREE RIVERS SERIES
NEW SONG SERIES
BANCROFT SERIES
MAGNOLIA SISTERS SERIES
SCARLETT SERIES
WILEY BROTHERS SERIES
PRYCE SISTERS SERIES
THE JACKSONS SERIES

ABOUT THE AUTHOR

Books have always been a big part of life for Jamaican born Brenda Barrett, she reports that she gets withdrawal symptoms if she does not consume at least two books per week. That is all she can manage these days, as her days are filled with writing, a natural progression from her love of reading. Currently, Brenda has several novels on the market, she writes predominantly in the historical fiction, Christian fiction, comedy and romance genres.

Apart from writing fictional books, Brenda writes for her blogs blackhair101.com; where she gives hair care tips and fiwibooks.com, where she shares about her writing life.

You can connect with Brenda online at:
Brenda-Barrett.com
Twitter.com/AuthorWriterBB
Facebook.com/AuthorBrendaBarrett

Chapter One

"**I** always thought you would get married before Mason." Ace's aunt Janet looked at him slyly. "Not one of Celia's three boys have made it to the altar. I am not implying that there is anything wrong with you, of course. But still…"

She sighed heavily. "Is your brother Trey still fooling around with that prostitute?"

Ace inhaled and counted silently to ten, Janet had no filter; she was his mother's oldest sister and the family busy body. Though these days, she wasn't as mobile as she used to be having broken three of her toes in a freak accident involving her cat.

He was the one who had picked the short straw to visit her and check the progress of her healing. His father, Ace Sr., had flatly refused to attend to her because of something Janet said that had caused them to have a falling out. That, unfortunately, was nothing new.

"I don't know what is going on in Trey's love life at

the moment." Ace answered, hoping his voice sounded unbothered.

Janet glanced at him contemplatively. "I won't even ask about Deuce since he broke up with Kelsey, he has been drifting through life like a straw on the sea. No one to replace her, and she is not coming home. It's quite sad."

"Straw on the sea?" Ace murmured, "I haven't heard that description before."

He unwrapped the bandages and inspected her toes; they were swollen and slightly purple.

"It hurts," Janet groaned, "am I going to lose my foot?"

"I doubt it," Ace looked at her, "what happened?"

"Someone may have stepped on it at Mason's reception last night. It was throbbing all night."

"You were told to take better care of them." Ace muttered, "they were almost better."

"But I had to dance with George Brady," Janet fluttered her eyelashes, "he is a lovely man. He can't really dance, and he kept stepping on my poor toes, but I didn't have the heart to tell him to stop."

"Here comes husband number two," Ace chuckled.

"What's wrong with that? Janet mumbled, "he is a widower, I am a widow. Both of us are lonely. The only issue is he doesn't want to live in Kingston, and I am not going back to Portland to live. I don't like the countryside."

"Well, that is a stalemate, no husband two for you then." Ace finished dressing her toes and stood up. "You are going to have to keep off them for at least the week."

"Oh well," Janet shrugged, "that's what you get for a night of fun. At my age, nights of fun are few and far between. I had to cease it while I could."

"How will you get around the house?" Ace frowned. Janet was a retired music teacher and an empty nester.

"Maybe you should ask one of the girls to come by."

"Oh no, "Janet shook her head, her chin-length silver hair glistened in the weak sunlight streaming through the floor to ceiling windows in her living room. "I love my children and grandchildren, but I prefer them in tiny doses. I'll be fine. I will hop around. I have Mavis, who comes by Monday, Wednesday, and Friday, and I have my stick."

"Okay, if you are sure," Ace packed up his bag and headed to the bathroom off the living room to wash his hands.

"Well, I have a little favor to ask of you, my favorite nephew." Janet hopped to the bathroom door and watched him. "I am renting out the garage apartment, since Nigel left it has been empty, and I promised George Brady that his daughter could rent it. Luckily, I hadn't let it out to anyone yet.

"George said she has been bunking with friends of his and feeling very uncomfortable, and that made him pretty sad. So I told him about my garage suite. She has the privacy, a separate entrance, and I did ask Mavis to go up there and stock the fridge with the basics."

"That's nice." Ace glanced at his aunt as she rambled on, "what's the favor?"

"I would be eternally grateful if you could make sure that everything is in order, show her around. I can't climb the stairs, or you know I would. I asked Mavis to clean up there within an inch of its life. So I am sure it is clean because she knows my exacting standards. Give her the tour for me, please. I want her to be happy here."

"When is she moving in?" Ace dried his hands and then glanced at his watch. He didn't have anything else to do until five o'clock. Today was supposed to be his lightest day. He usually did his rounds at Golden Acres in the evening.

A car horn blew at the front gate.

"That's her." Janet hopped to the front window and almost tripped over the cat again. She opened the curtain and whistled.

"She has grown into a beauty, but then again, what would one expect from her parentage. She looks a lot like her mom, Charlotte, the harlot. Charlotte slept with anything that could move."

"Aunt Janet," Ace said, warningly, "don't call people names or denigrate their character like that."

"It's like telling me not to tell the truth," Janet snorted, "Charlotte was the Biblical equivalent to Gomer and George the Hosea. Every time that woman strayed, he went back for her. The last time he picked her up, she was pregnant and living with Micky Wiley, but George took her back with the pregnancy and gave the child his name and treated her just like his. She's the youngest. I don't think any of the children are even his."

"Did you say, Micky Wiley?" Ace stiffened.

"Yup." Janet chortled, "that girl could be Micky Wiley's child. As well as not, who knows, her mother had a go-around with any man who could walk."

Ace looked through the window on the girl and gasped. She was pretty, cinnamon brown skin, thick curly hair that she had in an unkempt ponytail, perfectly shaped eyebrows, and pink lips. No makeup, she looked fresh-faced and young, slightly puffy around the eyes though as if she hadn't slept for a while. She could be anywhere in her twenties.

"George had her staying with some church friends of his in less than perfect accommodations." Janet murmured. "She looks fresh out of the country and as naïve as a newborn lamb. George kept the girls under tight security and made them dress like destitute nuns. You can understand why he didn't want any of them to be like the mother. You are going to have to keep an eye out for her."

"Me?" Ace whispered. "I don't have any time for that."

"Help your old aunt. I can't do it. I am barely mobile," Janet said, "show her around. It will take her a while to acclimatize to the place. Kingston is tiny compared to other cities, but it is still a city. She is used to cows and bleating goats and miles and miles of rolling countryside, not the fast-paced bustle that is Kingston."

"What is her name?" Ace asked.

"Kiya Brady," Janet hopped to the door, "I must greet her, the poor thing looks like she is about to cry."

Ace watched as the taxi man dumped Kiya's bags at her feet, all three of them, she obviously traveled light.

She paid for the taxi and then looked at the door again. Janet opened it just in time before her apprehension could turn into panic. Kiya slumped her shoulders in relief when the doors opened. He thought he saw her whisper, thank God.

"Hello, dear. Come on up." Janet called from the door. "I am afraid I can't come to help you."

Ace walked behind his aunt, belatedly realizing that he should offer his assistance. He was so busy looking at Kiya and her obvious relief to be there that he hadn't moved.

"Don't worry about the bags. My nephew will help." Janet smiled. "The neighborhood is fairly good; I doubt they'll rob you in less than a minute."

Ace walked to the door, and his eyes connected with Kiya's, neither of them moved.

"Ace," Janet whispered fiercely under her breath, "don't you dare like that girl. Don't you dare be attracted to this woman."

"Why?" Ace whispered back.

"You know why," Janet said, looking at him meaningfully. "She could be Micky Wiley's daughter, and if she is, don't let me say it out loud…"

"What are you talking about, Aunt Janet?" Ace looked at Janet guiltily. He knew what she was implying, and for a moment, he didn't care.

"You know what I am talking about," Janet said below her breath. "Just in case you are still unclear about it. Micky Wiley was your mother's gardener. You look a little bit too much like Micky Wiley for anyone to be comfortable. Come to think of it, your mother was not very much unlike Charlotte in that regard."

"All of that is just rumor and conjecture." Ace whispered, he glanced at Kiya was watching him and his aunt furiously whispering a tentative smile on her face.

"Please do not repeat any of this nonsense to anyone, especially Kiya."

Janet looked at him and forced a smile. "Well, Ace, for the sake of politeness, I am going to let this go, but just remember denial is a horrible thing. And you can deny and hide your head in the sand all you want, but one day you are going to have to face the truth.

"Anyway, I need to go and get the keys. Show the young lady around. Don't get any ideas in my absence. Your conscience should tell you to keep your distance from this particular girl."

She left to get the keys, and Ace walked toward the gate to help Kiya.

"Sorry about that," Ace smiled at her, "my aunt and I had a little disagreement. My name is Ace."

He held his hand for her to shake it, and she wiped it on the side of her Jean skirt and shook it, smiling tiredly.

"My name is Kiya Brady. I am so happy that your aunt allowed me to stay. I was desperate."

Ace frowned. "Why were you desperate?"

"Because where I'm coming from was horrible. I was sleeping on the floor. I was almost desperate enough to go back to Portland, and that would have been major desperation."

Ace looked at her quizzically. "Why? What happened in Portland?"

Kiya sighed. "My sister, Gwendolyn, got married to my ex-boyfriend. It's all sorts of awkward at home now. They were living with my father until their place is ready. I just needed to escape."

"Here's the key," Janet interrupted when Ace was about to find out more about what sounded like an interesting situation.

Ace took up Kiya's bags. He could take up all three at once, the bags weren't heavy at all. Ace wondered how long she was planning to stay to escape her sister and her ex-boyfriend.

"The apartment is through that pathway." Janet pointed to a cobblestone walkway. "You don't have to open the garage doors to go up the stairs, there is a side door. It is a lovely one-bedroom suite. It is very quiet and peaceful here as far as it can be peaceful in Kingston. We have an active neighborhood watch, and of course, there is a security system."

Janet held out a piece of paper to Ace. "These are the codes, show Kiya how to arm and unarm the place."

"I wish I could show you around myself, but…" Janet pointed to her newly bandaged toes. "I damaged my toes again. But don't you worry, Ace has been up to the apartment before. He'll give you the tour."

"That's okay, Mrs. Forbes. I'm so thankful to be here, and I am so happy that my father went to the wedding yesterday. When I called him this morning to complain, he said you had a place I could stay."

"Call me Janet." Janet smiled, "Mrs. Forbes is so formal. I'm hoping that we can be good friends and neighborly with each other, your father's family and mine go way back."

Ace walked along the pathway. Kiya took the keys from Janet and walked behind him.

"It's nice here," she said, in awe. "It doesn't feel like a city at all, I love the garden."

Ace looked back. "My aunts and mom are all into gardening and floral arrangements. It's their thing."

"Oh, it's my thing too." Kiya smiled. "I have my degree in AgroSciences."

"You do?"

"Yes, I do," Kiya smile. "I'm the only one from my family to graduate from college, it is a big deal, my father has my certificate framed and hanging in the shop."

Ace chuckled. "Maybe he wanted to send a message to your other siblings."

"Maybe or he just wanted to express his relief that I actually finished." Kiya smiled. "I almost didn't. It was taking me too long to get the degree.

"We expanded the shop. We are more like a mini mart now, and we have a jerk center. It was hectic juggling that with school."

"I noticed the expansion." Ace said, "I didn't know that was your doing."

"It was me and my sister's idea, we wanted to modernize the place." Kiya grimaced. "But sometimes, Kav is not up to the work, she has sickle cell, and she gets tired easily. I had to work late most days. I missed some exams because of it, and I flunked some courses, and then I stopped going altogether. So school wasn't making any sense for me."

"But obviously, you took it up again." Ace said, "that's

admirable."

"All credit goes to my friend Lucia, she paid for my final year through the Farm Help Society. She knew I wouldn't want to waste the charity's money. She said, you do a whole year without stopping and get that degree, and I did."

Ace frowned. "The Farm Help Society, isn't that Guy Wiley's thing?"

"Not anymore," Kiya said. "Lucia is in charge of that charity now, and she does really good work with the people in the neighborhood. She is focusing on education."

"That's great." Ace stopped before the door. "I know Lucia quite well; we had a relationship of sorts. I mistakenly believed that she would choose me over Guy Wiley. Of course, I didn't know him well or how deep their bond went. It was a long time ago, though."

Kiya frowned. "I can't imagine Lucia without Guy. They seem so perfect together."

"I agree." Ace cleared his throat. He really didn't want to discuss how wrong he was about the Lucia and Guy situation at the time.

He showed Kiya how to arm and unarm the place. She learned very quickly.

"My grand-aunt had something similar at her house," Kiya said. "It was used to have us running scared when it went off. The irony was, without her hearing aid, my grandaunt couldn't hear it at all, so we would be running around like crazy people while she would just calmly sit there unaffected."

Ace laughed. "Well, if you just follow the steps here, you'll be fine. Just unarm it before it goes off."

He started up the stairs. "Why is it that I haven't met you before?"

It was surprising really. He thought he knew everybody in

that area of the valley. He hadn't even known that George had such a pretty daughter with a lively sense of humor.

He had liked Kiya almost instantly because she was attractive, but now, he realized that she was quite easy to talk to. They were talking as if they were old acquaintances. He couldn't recall when was the last time he had found that sort of combination with a woman he was attracted to.

"I was always working at my father's shop," Kiya said. "If you ever visited my father's shop, you would have found me there. I never went anywhere; it was just church or work."

"You were a homebody," Ace smiled. "well then, that's why I never saw you. I lived in the neighborhood for a year, and I have visited George's place. I remember being served by a tall, light-skinned girl who was grumpy, I think she even growled at me."

Kiya laughed, "that sounds like Kavina. She was probably having a bad day. Maybe I wasn't around that day, maybe I was at school ..."

"Such a pity, I never met you then." Ace said. "I think we would have been great friends by now."

Kiya looked at him and smiled. "Maybe...but you'd be into Lucia; you may not have given me a passing thought."

"I would have." Ace said, "trust me, I would."

"What were you doing in Port Antonio?" Kiya asked, trying the keys one by one in the door without success.

"I was wrapping up my father's practice, but in the interim got caught up in taking on his retiring partners patients. I loved living in the Rio Grande valleys, especially when it rained, there was this fresh smell to the air."

"You're a doctor?" Kiya looked stunned. "I was thinking more along the lines of model."

Ace laughed and followed her inside when she finally opened the door. "Model! I have not heard that for a while, people say that about my brothers, especially Trey, but never about me."

Ace placed the bags on the welcome mat just inside the door and turned on the light. "Well, here is home."

Kiya stood still, her eyes wide. "Wow. I didn't expect this. I was expecting it to be a cramped little space that I could barely turn around in. This is luxurious. Kav is not going to believe this when I tell her. I can't believe it!"

Ace walked into this spacious garage-apartment with its open floor plan and looked around. It was nicely done.

"Aunt Janet had her grandson living here," he said. "He lived here for some time while going to university, but he's now in Japan."

Kiya still had not closed her mouth. She wandered around the spacious floor, looking and rubbing her hands along the furniture. "I can't believe this."

Ace enjoyed her look of wonderment.

"Fully furnished, my own room, my own kitchen." Kiya opened the bedroom door and stood at the entrance. "At home I ended up having to share with Kav when Gwen moved in with Sylvester.

"The bed is huge!"

Ace watched her indulgently.

"Now this is prayers answered," Kiya said, "I am living the dream. Gwen would eat her heart out if she knew what was happening."

"So Gwen is the sister who married your ex?"

Kiya made a face. "Yes, that's the one."

"And she moved back in with your ex, into the house that you are living in currently. It sounds uncomfortable." Ace folded his arms, waiting to hear more.

"It was super uncomfortable," Kiya shuddered, "especially when they were kissing and acting lovey-dovey. He was my boyfriend for five years, and we were engaged. I mean, we were picking out dresses and stuff. Then he met my sister and three months later they were married. I didn't know if I should laugh or cry."

"Or thank God you missed a bullet." Ace murmured, "how long ago was that?

"Six months," Kiya sighed. "I just couldn't take it anymore, living with them."

"I can't imagine how you stayed for six months." Ace said.

"I had to," Kiya shrugged, "the house is located behind the shop. I worked at the shop; I was the one who managed the whole thing. If anyone was to leave, it should have been Gwen and her husband."

"What does your sister and your ex do?" Ace asked curiously.

"Gwen is a dressmaker, and Sylvester is a carpenter. He's very good at it too. You should see some of the pieces he's made."

Ace smiled, "It seems as if you still have a thing for him."

"No, not in the least. I think I feel more betrayed by my sister." Kiya headed for the fridge in the kitchenette. "Your aunt has this fully stocked. When she said she had everything fully furnished, I didn't expect to get food as well."

Kiya looked at him guiltily. "Sorry for chatting your ear off. I like to talk a bit too much, and I am a bit overwhelmed by all of this."

Ace smiled. "I don't think you talk too much, and that feeling of being overwhelmed will subside eventually."

Kiya made a face. "I don't know if I'll get used to it, but I hope to."

"So, what will you be doing here exactly?" Ace asked, "My aunt just said you wanted a place to live. Are you going to work here in Kingston?"

"Oh, yes." Kiya nodded. "At my lowest point, when I thought I couldn't stand a minute more of Gwen and Sylvester, Myrtle Wiley mentioned to my dad that Guy was going to need a manager for his farm store in Kingston because his old manager was leaving. My dad told me, and I called Lucia, who told Guy that I could do it, and here I am. I got the job."

Kiya sat down in the settee and grinned. "Now, this is comfortable."

She yawned and closed her eyes, "I know it's the middle of the day, but I could sleep right here."

She was obviously tired, and he needed to leave her to get some rest.

He searched her features for any hint of a Wiley and then stopped himself. What was he doing? Janet's little jib had gotten through to him and was working to inoculate him against Kiya, but a little part of him resisted.

He was instantly attracted to her; she was not only pretty; she had a sense of humor that he liked. He made up his mind not to let his aunt's doubts affect the potential for a relationship that could mean something.

"I am leaving my business card on the counter," Ace said out loud. "My cellphone number is written at the back, call me if you need a lift to work."

"Thank you, Ace," Kiya opened her eyes and smiled at him sleepily. "You are one in a million."

Chapter Two

Ace drove toward the medical complex, he had two patients for the day, and then he had to head up to Golden Acres to do his rounds with his patients up there.

He fretted about giving Kiya his business card. It was not like him to be second-guessing himself so much, but should he have offered to take Kiya to work? Should he expose himself to her more than was necessary? He liked her. Even the thought of her excited him. He felt like a teenage boy all over again.

Ace imagined Kiya battling the transportation system to reach the Wiley complex from Janet's place, and he grimaced. It was only logical that he helped her out. Janet lived on his way to work. It would be no effort for him to stop by and pick her up.

However, Janet's insinuations were still ringing in his head, they got more and more insistent the further he drove from her house.

He couldn't escape it. He shouldn't let Janet get to him, but it was not her fault really, she was just repeating the ugly rumor that was in his family for years.

There was no escaping the fact that he and his brother Deuce resembled the Wileys more than they did their own father. Complete strangers had pointed it out to him, and they were doing it more often lately.

He shouldn't have to be in this kind of predicament. A person should be certain about their paternity.

This was all his mother's fault. He thought about confronting her today, this minute. However, he knew it wasn't going to happen, at least not the way he imagined in his head. His mother was rarely receptive to such inquiries about his paternity.

And his father was there. She would be cagey and guarded.

He turned into the spacious complex and parked in his designated parking space beside his father's car.

He inhaled and let his breath out in a whoosh. He got out of the car and stretched.

The complex was relatively new. It was built by his cousin, Quade, two years ago, and had a variety of medical specialists practicing there. It was designed to be picturesque and tranquil and not to look like a collection of medical buildings. It could give a small hotel a run for its money. Each building had a doctor or two occupying the space. He shared a building with his father, Ace Jackson Sr., they were both general practitioners; it was only logical that they shared the same space.

Trey was the only one who did not work in the complex. Trey was a general surgeon, and he practiced at Sunrise Medical, the posh private hospital run by Lucas Lawson, that looked even better than this complex.

Ace had often wondered if he should have joined his

brother over there instead of sticking with his father, but he had most of his father's patients now, so there was no going back.

Usually, his dad didn't work on a Monday.

His father had met mellowed a bit in the past couple of years. He called himself semi-retired and was occupying himself writing an extensive autobiography that actually made for entertaining reading. He had led quite a colorful life growing up in rural Jamaica.

What was worse these days his father had also become inexplicably interested in his life.

Ace groaned. His father had not been very close to him when he was growing up, but now in his semi-retired state, he seemed to have become a different man. He was seeking a connection that Ace still found to be a novelty. He wasn't used to his dad popping over to his house, wanting to watch a movie together, or discussing the newest chapter of his autobiography.

He knew his father was interested in his life before, but not to these semi-retired levels. While growing up, Ace and Deuce always knew that Trey was the favorite.

Maybe because Trey resembled their father quite a bit. Ace and Deuce resembled each other, and the Wileys, and they were born in Portland.

It all came back to Portland and Micky Wiley, the giant elephant in the room. Was that why he always felt as if something was missing between him and his father in the past.

His father had never mentioned the paternity doubt, but that didn't mean he had not thought about it.

He could remember the early days when his mother was the full-time parent, and his father was the one who just dropped by, though they lived in the same house. He was usually too tired to have any meaningful contact with them.

Was that by design or not?

One had to wonder if his father had been working through the knowledge that he was not their biological father. Obviously, he had made peace with it, but Ace hadn't.

Was he a Wiley or not? Was he entitled to the Junior at the end of his name? He had his father's full name, Ace Norman Jackson Jr.

Nobody called his father, Ace. Everybody called him Norman.

"Ace!" His father walked toward him from the office.

Ace waved. As usual, he searched his father's features these last few years since the doubt was planted in his mind about him being related to Micky Wiley.

He tended to look for similarities between him and his dad. As usual, he came up blank. There were no similarities at all. Well, maybe…he could say that they were both tall. His father was six-one. He was six.

His father had nutmeg brown skin, curly hair, a nose that flared slightly at the nostrils, generous lips, and eyes the color of brown sugar.

He, on the other hand, was a shade or two darker than his father, had the hooded Wiley eyes, had a straight as an arrow nose. Maybe they had the same hair?

Ace looked at his father's hair and almost felt his, even though it was cut low enough to be almost bald.

He was being ridiculous. He could put an end to this at any time. Why was he prolonging this nonsense?

A DNA test would clear all of this up, but his mother had forbidden him to even think of it. His mother had always gushed that he was her obedient child, and she had asked him to lay off the paternity question, and he had agreed.

He couldn't turn back now and dishonor his mother's

wishes. Or could he? Was it fair of her to ask it of him?

"I didn't expect to see you here," Ace Sr. said, "I thought you partied hard last night and would take a break today."

"Nope," Ace said, "I woke up at my usual time, I didn't party as hard as you older people. Besides, I had a couple of appointments to fulfill, and I went to see Aunt Janet."

Ace Sr. smirked. "What is your lovely Auntie up to?"

"She hurt her foot last night."

"Ahhh," Ace Sr. said sarcastically. "I knew she would. I wanted to warn her, but I was so busy socializing with everybody else."

"You took an oath to do no harm," Ace chuckled. "You saw a sister harming herself. You should have done something."

"And that is why I stayed away," Ace Sr. grinned. "I cannot take one more minute of Janet. I need some time to regain my equilibrium around her."

"What did you two fight about this time?" Ace asked.

"She's a busy body know-it-all," Ace Sr. smirked. "And I can't stand her, never could, never will."

"Weren't you her boyfriend many eons ago before you met Mom?" Ace chuckled, "at least you could have tolerated her then."

"She was different then." Ace Sr. scoffed, "and this time she went too far. Well, she kind of implied that..."

He paused, and then he sighed. "Sometimes she gets to me, you know."

"What did she imply?" Ace straightened up from the car.

"That something was wrong with all my sons, that's why not one of you is in a relationship." Ace Sr. sighed. "Usually, these things don't get to me, but I must admit I was thinking the same thing. She hit me on a raw nerve. When I was your age, Ace, I had two sons."

Ace inhale and then exhaled. "Nothing happens before the time."

"I know," Ace Sr. said contemplatively, "but I've thought about it, and I am prone to blaming myself. What's wrong with you boys? Is it something I did? Was it because you spent your formative years in your mother's care almost exclusively? Was it that we never presented a good relationship example, and that's why you are not into commitment?"

"It's none of the above," Ace said. "I think what you and Mom have is admirable. You've been together for forty years. In my case, I just haven't found the person I want to spend forty years with yet. Well, I may have, but…"

"You have someone in mind?" Ace Sr.'s face lit up. "Who is it?"

"It's too soon to say," Ace chuckled. "I just met her."

"That's how it worked with your mother and me." Ace Sr. said. "I saw her, and I knew. It's a feeling that is indescribable. You know what, I am going to help you out."

"Listen, Dad. I don't want any help with my love life."

"You are thirty-six, Ace. Apparently, you do. I want to have at least one grandchild before I die—Ace Jackson, the third."

"Good heavens! You are broody today."

"Weddings and funerals do that to me all the time, and Mason's wedding was a splendid reminder that there should be an Ace the third."

"I am going to blame Mason for this as soon as he gets back from his honeymoon." Ace muttered.

Ace Sr. laughed. "Your mother is waiting for you, she said she has something for you to take to Quade later."

****

Ace entered the receptionist area, which smelled more like

a spa than a doctor's office. That was his mother's doing. She believed that aromatherapy was beneficial to the patients waiting in the reception area.

He inhaled whiffs of lavender essential oil, he could also smell traces of bergamot and clary sage. It was supposed to relax and rejuvenate. His receptionist, Jessica, was at her desk. She looked relaxed. Maybe a bit too much. She looked at him sleepily. "Doctor Ace, your mother is in your office."

"Thank you, Jessica."

His mother was sitting at his desk with her laptop.

"Hello, my handsome son."

Ace set across from her and resisted rolling his eyes. Celia Jackson was still a pretty woman, and she knew it.

She was sometimes mistaken for much younger than she was. She had peanut buttery smooth skin, with nary a wrinkle in sight, naturally red pouty lips, and she was wearing her signature hairstyle.

He couldn't remember if his mother had ever changed that hairstyle, she had worn it like that for years. It was a bell cut that framed her face and was streaked with burgundy strands where he assumed her gray hairs would be. The greys were never allowed to see the light of day.

"What's wrong?" she asked. "You look troubled."

"I met somebody today," Ace said, watching her expression.

"Oh, you did. That's great, Ace."

"Her name is Kiya Brady."

"The name Brady rings a bell."

"George Brady's daughter. Aunt Janet said she was the youngest of George's children."

"Ah, that George Brady. Saw him yesterday at the wedding. Apparently, he was Celine's invite."

"No, I think it was Mason. He knows him very well and they still keep in touch."

Celia nodded. "Well, whatever. It was nice to see some of the old faces from Portland again. So you like his daughter, huh?"

"I do." Ace nodded. "Even though Aunt Janet said..."

"Your aunt Janet said what? Celia asked sharply, "that woman talks too much."

"She implied that Kiya was Micky Wiley's daughter." Ace watched his mother's expression closely.

Celia sighed a long, drawn-out sigh.

"Is it okay if I date her, mother?"

"You have never asked me that question before," Celia said uncomfortably. "I don't care who you date. I have never intervened in your love life or any of my other children. I didn't intervene with Deuce and his on again off again roller coaster ride with Kelsey. I never intervened when Trey took home a stripper to dinner and declared that he loved her beyond life itself. I am not about to intervene now."

"Did you hear what I said, Mom? She may be Micky Wiley's daughter."

"And why should that matter? Celia asked. "You are Ace Jackson, Jr. I am tired of the same old conversation. You are not a Wiley; you are a Jackson. Micky was a handsome man, every woman wanted to get with him..."

"Including you?" Ace asked.

"I am not going to answer that," Celia snorted, "Never. Your aunt, Janet, is getting to be too much."

"Mom, can we concentrate on the conversation at hand and not Aunt Janet, as bad as she is."

"She took a rumor, made it into the truth, and now you're making my life hell!" Celia growled. "Why shouldn't I be talking about Janet?"

"I would prefer if we talk about Micky Wiley," Ace

said."And I would prefer not to," Celia said mutinously. "Now, can I give you the package for Quade?"

"What is it?" Ace sighed.

"It's a whole thing of mangoes. I picked them from the tree at the front." Celia said, sounding disgusted with him. "Quade loves his East Indian mangoes."

"Okay," Ace sighed. "All right, Mom. I'll allow this change of subject."

Celia made a face. "I wish you would allow it forever, and never mention this nonsense again."

"But you heard what I said, Mom. I like this girl, Kiya, and I'm going to pursue her. Do I have your blessing?"

"I don't know this girl," Celia said. "I can't give my blessing unless I meet her."

Ace nodded. "Very well."

Chapter Three

The phone woke her up. There was an incessant ringing in the background of her sleep. It finally jerked her out of her slumber. Kiya opened her eyes. She didn't know where she was. The feeling of disorientation lasted for a good minute, and then she realized that she was at Janet's place.

She was no longer staying at the Hawthorns, and she had met Ace Jackson.

She fell asleep thinking about Ace Jackson. He was talking, and he said something about leaving his number on the counter, and she didn't remember anything else.

Well, except the part where he said he'd drop her to work tomorrow. Tomorrow or was it today?

It was dark outside. Probably it was the same evening. She was so bone-tired, she didn't even remember.

She didn't even know where the light switches were. She stumbled around in the dark. Finally, she found one. She closed her eyes because the brightness was like pinpricks against her lids. Her phone rang again, and she saw her handbag on the center table. She made a leap for it. She didn't want whoever it was to stop calling. It was her dad.

"Hey Kiya. I've been trying you all evening. Where were you?"

"At Janet's. I fell asleep in the couch."

"Hmm," George mused. "You deserve it. You worked so hard when you were here, and now you're going to just work again. No vacation."

Kiya chuckled. "I can't afford a vacation, Dad." She spotted a clock near the kitchen and gasped. "It's two o'clock in the morning."

"Yes," George muttered, "just locked up the shop. You know how it goes."

"Yes, I know," Kiya mumbled. And she didn't miss it. Not while Sylvester and Gwen were there.

"So, how is the place?" George asked. "Janet said it was big and spacious."

"It is very nice. It looks like something out of a magazine. Janet has wonderful taste."

"You are not going to want to come back home," George said regretfully. "I thought you'd see how busy Kingston was and then decide to come back."

"Not going to happen," Kiya snorted. "I can't stand home at the moment."

"I understand," George said mournfully, "but you were the only reliable help I had."

"Kav said she'd help out more," Kiya said.

"Kav is in and out of the hospital lately and not much use to me here. Besides, she's miserable, I don't want her interfacing with the customers regularly. Everybody who comes into the shop asks for you longingly."

Kiya laughed. "She's not miserable. She's just grumpy."

"Oh, yes, she is miserable," George snorted. "I can't stand it when Kav gets into one of her moods. I stay far away. If I could tolerate Kingston, I would come and join you. Just so I can escape that girl."

"Her sickle cell makes her unhappy," Kiya said, defending Kav. "It can't feel right being always in pain."

Kiya cleared her throat. "How are Gwen and Sylvester? I bet they are happy that I am gone."

"They had a quarrel last night," George said. "they went out and came back; both of them looked unhappy. Gwen was crying in the night. She slept out in the living room. I don't see them lasting two years if they continue like this."

"You think so?" Kiya asked enthusiastically.

"It pains me to say it," George said. "Gwen is my child, but both of them are selfish. It's hard to make a relationship work with two selfish people. Somebody has to give."

"I don't think I wish them ill," Kiya mused. "I just can't believe the two of them went behind my back like that."

"It wouldn't have been easy even if they didn't," George sighed. "heartbreak is a part of life, my dear Kiya. Anyway, I'm going to leave you now and let you get some rest."

"Thanks for calling, Dad," Kiya yawned.

George chuckled. "See, you need that rest."

When he hung up, Kiya settled back in the settee and closed her eyes.

Last year around this time, she had been planning her wedding to Sylvester. She was so naive. She thought that everything was going to be all flowers and music and fairy tales. It was a long engagement, but she didn't mind. They had agreed that she needed to finish school first, and Sylvester, who had inherited a piece of land with a ramshackle house on it would refurbish the house. They would live together and have babies. She had imagined a son with Sylvester's cute babyface features and a girl who looked like a cross between them.

And then Gwen had moved back home. She had moved out years before to live in Port Antonio, where she secretly lived with her boyfriend. She hadn't wanted their father to find out because he would insist on marriage, and the guy was already married.

When Gwen moved back in, it hadn't taken two weeks before Sylvester was panting at Gwen's feet. Gwen had that effect on men. It was understandable. She had the kind of shape that the men in the community drooled over. She had generous breasts, a high round bottom, and a tiny waist that looked like she wore corsets twenty-four hours a day. Added to the glorious shape, she had exotic features.

She had medium brown skin, with grey eyes and naturally long eyelashes that looked like mini fly swatters.

Two bats of her eyelashes a come-hither smile and her ever-present straight weave that she was always tossing over her shoulders, and Sylvester was a goner. He had protested after Kiya chastised him for lusting after her sister.

"Listen, I am not into women who wear tons of makeup and have long, fake nails." He had said piously, "I prefer the natural look. I think you are better looking than Gwen."

But his eyes would follow Gwen when she wore her skimpy tight shorts around the house, and he would swallow convulsively when she bent to pick something up, and Gwen always seemed to be bending down to pick up something when Sylvester was around.

Kiya should have known that the writing was on the wall when she was at the shop, and Sylvester would eagerly offer to go over to the house to wait for her. He had started coming around more frequently, and he was always hurrying off when she showed up.

Kavina, her other sister was the one who had pointed out what was going on behind her back.

"I saw Gwen and Sylvester going at it, in your bed," Kavina said without sugar-coating it. "While you were waiting for marriage to do the deed, Gwen has no such moral standards. I told Gary that if he looked at her twice, I was going to pluck out his eyes."

Gary was the chef at the jerk center they had just opened and Kavina's boyfriend.

Kiya had stood looking at Kavina, confused. "What do you mean going at it?"

"Piston action, clothes off, moaning," Kavina said flatly.

Kavina had a way of talking that was monotonous. Her voice, at the best of times, had no emotion. Her little list of words, irritated Kiya so much that she felt like shaking her. The images it brought to mind was heartbreaking.

"Don't shoot the messenger," Kavina said, seeing how she was seething. "I just deliver the news."

She had confronted Sylvester the same evening, she had gone to his parent's house. A place that was always noisy and crowded with children.

And accosted him in the middle of the yard.

He hadn't denied it, he had looked at Kiya guiltily. "I am sorry, Kiya, but when you know she's the one, you know. There is no need to wait on love, and I love her, it's not the kind of love I have for you, this is like a fever in my blood, I'd do anything for her."

Kiya was going to argue. She was prepared to kick up a stink that the neighborhood had never seen before, but she had looked into Sylvester's eyes and realized something— he wasn't worth it. There must be someone in the world for her who wouldn't fall for Gwen's obvious charms. She had thought that they had something more than lust.

However, she was delusional. Her favorite song was Marcia Griffith's Dreamland; maybe she had listened to it too much and had cast Sylvester into her fantasy.

Four weeks after that incident, Sylvester and Gwen were married. It was a small affair in Sylvester's yard. Gwen sewed her own gown; her father paid for and kept the reception at the shop.

Kiya had not gone to either event. However, Kavina attended both affairs and gave her the report.

"They looked good together," Kavina said, "her dress fit her like a dream. The food was good, and his family gobbled it up like they had never seen food before. There were quite a few of them, and they were all hungry," Kavina had shuddered. "It's a good thing, Dad, over catered."

Following the wedding, Gwen moved out to live with Sylvester in the grungy back room that he had at his parents' house. Three weeks later, she was back with him in tow.

She couldn't deal with the conditions, and Sylvester couldn't spend a day without her. Her father, ever the big softie, allowed them to stay.

It was so insensitive. She had been seeing the guy for five years, thought she was going to marry him and here he was living in her father's house with her sister.

She couldn't bear the sympathy and knowing looks from her regular customers. Though that was easier than spending time at home. To her, it was an untenable situation.

So when Myrtle said that Guy was looking for a manager, Kiya had been quick to cease it as an escape route. She had been to Kingston once when she was a little girl for a church function and had thought about it as a big busy place that was too hectic for her. Still, she was sure that working in Kingston was something she could do, anything was better than home.

She had called Lucia Wiley as soon as she heard about the vacancy. It was perfect timing because Lucia had been in New York and had just returned. Lucia was appalled at the turn of events in her life.

She was sure Lucia convinced Guy to hire her immediately because she didn't even have to do an interview.

Now the job was hers, and she started tomorrow.

The outgoing manager, Marlene Lovett, had agreed to stick around for a few weeks to help her in the new role.

Thank God for small blessings, because she did not know one thing about managing a farm store. However, she figured it couldn't be that hard, she managed her father's shop for years; a farm store shouldn't be that different.

She headed for the room with her bags.

She hadn't even tried out the bed yet. There were a few things she needed to do. Find an outfit for tomorrow, make sure it was ironed and then find some appropriate work clothes. Where did one go to buy clothes here, she had no idea, she would have to ask Lucia.

She would also need to discuss the rent with Miss Janet. She had no idea how much it was, and she would need to call Ace Jackson to pick her up tomorrow and find out about the bus system and taxi system after this.

She could not be depending on Ace Jackson to be picking her up. He was a doctor, not a taxi man.

She yawned widely. Yes, she had some sleep left in her. She set her phone to alarm at 6:30 and got into bed, and close their eyes, smiling when she thought about Ace.

When she had first seen him, she had stopped and stared in awe. She couldn't believe that someone like him existed for real. It was not every day you saw a man with chiseled features and dreamy, hooded eyes.

He reminded her of someone, but she couldn't quite place

who it was.

She wondered vaguely if he liked her, but why would he? She was just an average country-bumpkin.

Men like Ace probably went for the Gwendolyn's of this world. She gritted her teeth when she thought of her sister.

It was hard growing up with a sister who was so-called exotic, everyone always commented on her eyes and her long curly hair.

Of her parent's four children, Gwendolyn was definitely the standout. Her brother, Lorenzo, the oldest, was tall, lanky, and average. Gwen followed him, and she was the beauty, Kavina had slightly slanted eyes that gave her a cat-like quality, and then there was Kiya, average. She didn't have any outstanding qualities. Nobody would stop traffic for her or had a fire inside that they couldn't quench.

She was a medium in every way—complexion, weight, clothes size. Men like Ace didn't go for medium, neither did men like Sylvester, apparently.

She closed her eyes, willing herself not to think of how jealous she was of her above-average sister and bemoaning things that she couldn't change.

The Serenity Prayer came to mind.

"God grant me the serenity to accept the things I cannot change..." She smiled to herself.

People always wished for what they didn't have. That's for sure.

Chapter Four

Kiya got up promptly at sixty thirty feeling rested. She had a shower, changed into what she thought would be suitable work clothes, and was just contemplating what to have for breakfast when Janet rang her.

"Come on over for breakfast, Kiya. I have too much. I need to share."

Kiya didn't want to refuse. She couldn't refuse. She needed to speak to Janet about the rent.

It was a short walk to the main house over cobblestones that were lined with colorful bougainvillea. The back door was open, and she walked right in.

"Come on in, come on in," Janet called. "What time do you have to get to work?"

"I'm supposed to report there for nine," Kiya said, looking around. Janet's place was light, airy, and uncluttered. It was her kind of style.

Obviously, Miss Janet was not old-school like her father.

Her father loved his red velvet settees and crotchet pieces on
every arm and his bamboo separators that jingled when you
walked through them, not to mention the figurines on every
available shelf in the living room.

Kiya liked the light colors, the neutrals, and the fact
that Janet's place was uncluttered. She looked around
appreciatively.

"I have green bananas, callaloo, and orange juice," Janet
said jovially. "You won't be hungry until lunchtime."

Kiya sat at the island and watched as Janet hobbled from
one end of the room to the next.

"Do you want any help?"

"No, thank you, deary, I can manage." Janet served the
food in platters and place them at the table. "Come along.
Let's eat."

Kiya sat across From her. "Ah, Miss Janet."

"Just Janet, dear," Janet said smiling.

"About the rent…"

"Rent!" Janet opened her eyes. "You couldn't afford to live
over my garage in this part of Kingston. It's a fully furnished,
spacious one bedroom, living room, kitchen... As long as you
pay the utility bills, they will come in Nigel's name, you'll
be fine."

Kiya opened her mouth and then closed it. "Thank you.
Thank you so much."

"No problem, dear." Janet smiled with her. "I really like
the fact that I have company. I miss having Nigel around,
even if we didn't talk every day, or we didn't interact. I knew
he was here, and I felt comfortable.

"I don't particularly like people in my space, and I'm pretty
sure as a young person, you wouldn't want an old lady with
her nosy self in yours, would you?"

Kiya grinned. "Ah, no, I wouldn't. It's nice to have the

space to myself."

"Good. Then we have it settled, then. You pay your water, light, internet... the telephone is disconnected, but you have your cell phone. You'll be fine. Your father said you are the most responsible of his four children."

Kiya nodded. "Dad always says that."

"Tell me about your siblings." Janet queried. "I can recall there's a boy and three girls."

"Yes, my brother Lorenzo works on a ship."

"As in cruise ship?" Janet raised an eyebrow.

"Yes." Kiya nodded. "He's hardly home."

"He was the first one, wasn't he?" Janet tucked into her breakfast, "how old was he again?"

"Thirty," Kiya said.

"And he was followed by that pretty sister of yours, she had big grey eyes. She looked like a doll. What's her name again?"

Kiya barely held back a grimace. Everybody thought Gwen looked like a doll.

"You mean, Gwendolyn?" She hoped her voice didn't leak out any of the resentment she was feeling. "Yes, she follows Lorenzo, she's twenty-eight."

"What is she doing with herself?"

"She is a dressmaker." Kiya made a face. "She's very good too. She got married the other day."

"Ah," Janet nodded, "to your fiancé."

"My dad told you?" Kiya asked.

"Oh, yes," Janet nodded. "And that is why I was so willing to let you stay here. I understand how that feels."

"You do?" Kiya asked.

"Oh, I do," Janet nodded. "My sister married the man that I loved, but he loved her. She was the pretty one. Don't worry about it; eventually, you'll forget all of this madness. You'll find someone, and you'll ask yourself, what did I see in that guy?"

"Thank you, Miss Janet, er… Janet." Kiya nodded. "Thank you."

Janet smiled. "So after Gwendolyn comes the grouchy one. What's her name again?"

"Kavina," Kiya said, smiling at the description of her sister.

"I always liked the name Kavina. How is Kavina these days? I know she's sickly."

"She has good days and bad days," Kiya murmured. "She helps my dad out at the shop, and she is debating whether to marry her childhood boyfriend, Greg. He loves her and doesn't mind her… er… grouchiness."

Janet nodded and looked at her contemplatively. "You look so much like your mother. She was a pretty girl, Charlotte Bigby. Do you remember her?"

"Only vaguely and I am not sure if they were real memories," Kiya said. "I was four when she died."

"She died in childbirth, didn't she?" Janet sighed. "It was a tragic case."

Kiya nodded. She didn't really remember her mom. She only knew how she looked from pictures. Her father said her mother was always running away, and when she was younger, her mother was not around.

"I hope you're nothing like her," Janet said softly. "Nothing at all."

Kiya cleared her throat. "Excuse me?

"Your mother, she couldn't settle down."

"I heard," Kiya said sadly. "My dad rarely talks about it, but since I'm an adult, I could figure that she was that way." Kiya looked at her watch. "I will have to go soon. I texted Ace to pick me up."

Janet frowned. "You can't get involved with Ace, you

know. I am almost sorry I introduced you two. I saw the way you looked at each other. I can't allow this to happen."

"Why," Kiya snorted "because he's a doctor?"

"Goodness, no!" Janet said dryly, "I am not a snob. I can't afford to be snobbish, I'm from humble roots. Ace is from humble roots. We are all from Portland, and that is my point. We are all from the same place."

Kiya looked at Janet, confused. "I don't understand."

"I wish I could explain it," Janet said heavily. "I wish I didn't have to say this, but stay away from Ace, please, as a favor."

"He's probably on his way to pick me up." Kiya felt a little hurt by Janet's insistence that she stay away from her nephew.

"I know, I know," Janet sighed. "I'll look into giving you Nigel's car to drive. You can drive, can't you? I know George taught all his children to drive."

"Yes, I can drive." Kiya was once again totally confused. "I used to pick up stuff for my father for the shop all the time."

"Well, then. I'll have to work out the insurance issue on Nigel's vehicle and see if you can get it. That way. You won't have to depend on Ace to take you anywhere, and you can drive to and from work. When you go with him today, pay attention to the route. I'll ask my daughter to get it licensed and insured. You should get it by the end of the week."

"But," Kiya paused. "I don't know what to say."

"Trust me on this, Kiya," Janet said. "I know what I'm doing. I know why I said you should stay away from Ace Jackson. I don't want to see you hurt. You have had enough in your young life to deal with already."

Chapter Five

Ace was at Janet's gate promptly at seven forty-five. He had gotten Kiya's text earlier that morning, and he was only too eager to see her again. He had been up anyway and swimming in the newly installed pool.

That would be his exercise today. He had a full schedule ahead. He had forgotten that he and his brothers were scheduled to sing at a charity event later that evening.

He got out of the car and ran inside to check on Janet to see how her foot was getting on. Kiya met him at the door.

"I gave Kiya breakfast," Janet said. "Such a sweet girl. Such a pity she is family." Janet asked cheekily.

Ace wasn't listening. He was looking at Kiya, who seemed a little different today. Maybe because she was in a fitted blouse and pants that hugged her curves.

He thought Janet said she dressed just like a nun. If that were true yesterday, it wasn't true now.

"Oh, Ace! I'm going to get my bag," Kiya's face lit up.

"You look pretty today," Ace said. "Not that you didn't look pretty yesterday, but wow."

Janet frowned at him. "Ace Jackson."

Ace grinned. "Well, Aunt Janet, I'm happy to see that you're not worst off. I'll come and check on you tomorrow."

"About that," Janet said, "I think I'm going to ask Ace Sr. to take over my care."

"He doesn't want to have anything to do with you," Ace grinned. "I'll wait in the car, Kiya." He turned toward the door.

Kiya didn't take long to come inside the car. She had a troubled expression on her face.

"What's wrong?" Ace asked.

"I am puzzled about your aunt Janet. She said something quite weird earlier."

"Aunt Janet is pretty strange when she's ready." Ace grinned. "I would suggest that you don't pay her any mind."

"She said I should stay away from you and she was so adamant about it, she offered me Nigel's car."

Ace laughed. "Well, take the car. Nobody is driving it anyway. As for Janet, ignore her." He drove down the avenue and into traffic. "I'm going to make a brief stop at my office. My brothers and I have an appointment at a charity event tonight. Trey just dropped off the soundtrack, I am going to have to practice when I run up to Golden Acres today."

"You guys sing?" Kiya asked excitedly. "The singing doctors?"

"It's somewhat of a family tradition." Ace grinned. "And yes, we do sing. We've been singing since we were toddlers.

"My mom's family had a tradition of it. You see, my grandfather was a meteorologist, and his name was Ray. My grandmother's name was Sunny, and he named all his children the names of hurricanes, so they called themselves

Sunny Ray and the Hurricanes."

"I know about that group," Kiya said. "The older folks at church always talk about Sunny Ray and the Hurricanes. You guys were a staple at church fairs and nine nights."

"Not you guys," Ace grinned. "I wasn't around then. I'm not that old."

"How old are you?"

"Thirty-six," Ace said.

"It's nice that you have a close relationship with your brothers." Kiya mused. "I wish I had a close relationship with my sisters, but I have never been close to mine, though I have tried, I just think it is a personality clash with the three of us. How are you and your brothers?"

"We're good," Ace said. "Deuce is laid back and cool. He's two years younger than I am. We play tennis most weeks, well not as much lately since he is filling in for a colleague at the children's hospital.

"And Trey, he's the baby of the family. He's a former playboy, he used to play the field hard. He just started getting serious about Christianity. He's even preaching now.

"Previously, it was just Duece and me. We used to be a duet. Now, we are a group, a trio. Ace, Deuce, Trey— one, two, three."

Kiya laughed. "Your mother must be very cool."

"She is." Ace chuckled. "Unfortunately, Deuce used to be teased about his name, so he doesn't like it. So he goes by DJ.

"Say Kiya, do you want to come to the charity event at my church later? It is a fundraiser for a sick child who needs specialized care off the island. This was Deuce's initiative."

"Sure," Kiya. "I'm all for that. I could even do an item."

"You sing?" Ace asked.

"I sing. I was the head of our praise and worship team at

my church. I used to lead out for all the worship services. It was my pleasure."

"Hmm." Ace chuckled, "Well, it seems as if I have the right girl here. I am going to set Solomon King on you. He always wants new members for the choir."

"I don't mind." Kiya chuckled. "I'm up for it. Well, I'll pick you up after work. What time does work end by the way."

"At five. Today is going to be light. The current manager is showing me the ropes for the next two weeks. And then it will just be me."

"I wish you all the best," Ace smiled. "I want you to do well and to stay here in Kingston."

Kiya held her breath when he turned all of that smile on her. He was a seriously handsome man.

Sylvester didn't hold a candle to Ace. She imagined herself going back home with Ace and rubbing it into Gwen's face.

Oh, here is my new boyfriend, she imagined herself saying. Gwen would be green with envy.

"My place is over here." Ace turned into a parking lot.

It looked more like a residence with palm trees and greenery and cobblestone walkways. There was a big billboard sign with several names on it, with their specialties. There were so many 'ologists' up there; she was becoming baffled reading through it. How was a neurologist different from a urologist or a pathologist and a radiologist?

The parking lot was already half-filled. Ace parked in a spot with his name on it, Ace Jr.

"I'll be back." He got out. "Just going to have a brief consultation with my brothers."

Shortly after he left the car, another vehicle drove up in the space marked Ace Sr.

Kiya looked over at the car interestedly. What was Ace Sr. like? She didn't have long to wait.

He alighted from the car, glanced over at his son's car, and then did a double take when he saw her.

"Good heavens, a girl." He slammed his car door and came over to her.

"And who is this beautiful creature?"

Kiya automatically smiled.

He was friendly and outgoing. A handsome older gentleman who still looked fit. He didn't slouch at all; he had a military-like bearing.

She was expecting Ace Sr. to look like a senior, as in old but he didn't.

"My name is Kiya Brady."

"Ah." Ace Sr. grinned. "Kiya Brady... Brady. Where have I heard Brady before?"

"Portland," Kiya said. "My father is George Brady. He owns the shop at the square."

"Ah," Ace Sr. laughed. "Georgie Brady! The Jacksons and the Bradys go way back."

"You do?" Kiya widened her eyes.

"Oh, yes. Back in the days," Ace Sr. leaned on his car, "the Bradys and the Jacksons were very close. We had lands adjoining each other. George and I went to the same school."

"You did?"

"Yes, we did." Ace Sr. chuckled. "Your father was quite the mathematician."

"I know." Kiya chuckled. "My dad does not let a dollar go missing when he's counting up the money. Every cent counts."

Ace Sr. laughed. "Yes, yes. That's George for you. He was quite the hustler when we were at school, he used to make things like coconut drops and gizzadas and sell them. He even took orders, so he had an idea of how many of what to make. It was not shocking to me that he went into retail."

"Oh really," Kiya chuckled, "Dad never really talks about his school days. I didn't know that."

"He should talk about it and not let it get lost in the quagmire of memories." Ace Sr. looked at her contemplatively, "that's why I am writing an autobiography. I am forcing myself to relive the memories, put them in perspective.

"I am only realizing lately that my childhood in Portland was not bad at all. It bordered on perfect. My brother and I used to run wild. My issue is putting all the info together, there are so many stories I don't even know where to start."

"Start at the beginning." Kiya nodded. "The very beginning—when you were born, where you were born, and then go from there."

"That's the thing," Ace Sr. said. "My very beginning is quite interesting. I had to stop and do some research into it, separate some fact from fiction."

"How is that?" Kiya asked curiously.

Ace Sr. chuckled. "Well, my mother was a respectable nurse, and was active in her church; she had two children out of wedlock, so she invented a husband and named him Silas Jackson. He was supposed to have died at sea."

Kiya opened her mouth. "Really?"

"Really." Ace Sr. laughed. "That was what happened back in the day, you know? An unmarried nurse or teacher had to be above reproach."

Kiya frowned. "Unrealistic expectations, I'd say."

"That's true, but my mother maintained the fiction that she was Mrs. Silas Jackson till the day she died." Ace Sr. chuckled. "After a while, I think she even started believing her own fiction."

"That she was married, and her husband died at sea?"

"That's right," Ace Sr. laughed. "And then I grew up with my grandparents. They were herbalists, you know. It seems as if the medicine was in my blood. My grandparents were herbalists, my mother was a nurse, I became a doctor, and now all three of my sons are doctors. Ace Jr. is an excellent doctor and man."

"Kiya smiled. "I've kind of figured that out."

"This mistress, Medicine, can consume a man, but you cannot give up on Ace. He's a prince among men."

"Dad!" Ace interrupted his father's glowing description of him. "What are you telling Kiya?"

"Just helping you along with the courtship." Ace Sr. chuckled. "Don't mind me. Have a good day, Miss Kiya Brady. And give my regards to your father. I hope to see you soon."

"Kiya is coming to the charity concert tonight." Ace said, heading toward the driver's section of the car.

"Ah well, that makes my day." Ace Sr. winked at her.

"Sorry about him," Ace said when he started the car. "My dad is semi-retired and feeling mischievous these days."

Kiya laughed. "He wasn't only doing matchmaking. He was also telling me his story about Portland and the old days. He said he went to school with my father."

"Oh, is that so?" Ace said.

"He said that his mother made up a husband, just to hide the fact that she was a single mother."

"Oh," Ace looked at her. "That means my dad likes you. He never just blurts out that story to just anyone." Ace chuckled. "Whenever I hear the story, I wonder why no one ever questioned that she and her husband had the same surname. It seems a little convenient to me."

"I have a church friend who married a guy with the same surname." Kiya grinned. "And they were not related. They actually did a DNA test to make sure."

Ace looked at her when she said that, "that's interesting."

"I wonder who the fictional Mr. Silas Jackson was," Kiya mused. "Probably it was somebody in the neighborhood."

"Maybe." Ace glanced at her, "but whoever it was, we never had any indication who it was. She took the secret to her grave, and there lies my problem with these old secrets."

"Yes, it's frustrating for the ones left behind." Kiya sighed. "I like a good mystery, but I like it when it's solved."

"Some mysteries are better left as mysteries, I think," Ace said. "Or else knowing the outcome could hurt a lot of people."

"I don't agree with that." Kiya snorted. "It could help a lot of people. Some persons need to know what is going on in their family tree. For example, my sister Kavina has sickle cell. If my dad and mom knew that they were carriers, then this would be a different story. Sometimes I just hate to see her suffer. Her pain makes her miserable. She blames my dad for her pain since my mother isn't around."

"Why?" Ace asked.

"Sometimes, in the depths of her misery, she will ask him why he bothered having her." Kiya grimaced, "Kav suffers a lot with her disease and she is determined that Dad feels guilty for her suffering."

Ace cleared his throat. "Well, your father had no control over that."

"I think she sometimes wished that Gwen and I got sickle cell instead of her. Well, she has said as much. She said she just wants us to suffer for just one day so that we would know what it's like."

"Pain will make you say things." Ace smile. "But is she getting help for her condition?"

"Yes, she is." Kiya nodded. "The bulk of Daddy's funds go toward caring for her. He spends a lot of money on Kavina's health issues, that's why she hasn't married Gary, her high school sweetheart. She says he can't afford all of her expenses."

"She should be grateful she has a father that cares so much," Ace said. "So many of my patients don't have that kind of care and love. The charity event we're having this evening is for a boy who doesn't have a father who cares. His mother is all alone, and his medical condition is quite expensive and too much for us to handle out here. He has a rare disease."

"My dad has always cared," Kiya said. "I don't know what we'd do without him."

"Well, count your blessings," Ace smiled at her. He turned into what looked like a vast shopping center. She couldn't see the end of it, it was larger than what she was expecting. Instantly, a feeling of anxiety threatened to overtake her.

"And here you are. I hope you have a good day at work today," he said it softly.

Kiya looked at him and was mute for a while, she forgot that she was anxious.

"Thank you, doctor... Mr. Ace," She stuttered.

He grinned. "Pick you up at five."

Chapter Six

When Kiya heard 'farm store,' she didn't know what she was expecting. Certainly, it wasn't this modern-looking edifice, which was a part of a more extensive complex, all filled with different stores. It was on a scale that she had never seen before. Of course, she was a country-bumpkin, so that could account for her shock and awe. There was nothing approaching this kind of scale where she was from.

She walked into a spacious area with five cashiers and a variety of farm equipment and farm products on display.

She spoke to one of the cashiers at the front and asked for the manager, Marlene Lovett. She was sent to an office area at the back of the store. There was a long corridor with doors with signs on them, like kitchen, assistant manager, and then manager.

When she heard that she was going to be the manager for this place, she had thought it would have looked like her father's shop. At George's shop, you could see from one end to the other.

This was on another level.

She knocked on the door that said manager and heard a muffled, "Come in."

She pushed the door and was once again stunned, it was a spacious place, and she was struck by how bright it was.

Marlene Lovett sat behind a desk, but behind her was a greenhouse that could be seen through sizable windows. It was a large greenhouse designed like a courtyard. They even had a fishpond.

"Wow." Kiya paused, looking through the windows awestruck. "I didn't expect this.

"It is a lovely, unexpected view, isn't it?" Marlene chuckled. "You are early. You are Kiya, right?"

"Yes, I am." Kiya nodded.

"Well, have a seat," Marlene said, pointing to the chair in front of her desk. "I'll be with you in a minute. We are getting a new shipment of orchids today, and they'll be going into rehab, and I'll have to make sure that the guys have it right— soon be back. Don't go anywhere. I'll tell you all about rehab and all of that tomorrow, but right now, they're waiting."

Marlene left the office, and Kiya looked around. Marlene had a red and black theme going on, with pictures of strawberries and other plants. Kiya felt a shaft of excitement zing through her. She was going to love this office, and she was going to love working here. She could feel it. There was a picture of Marlene and her family on the desk. Kiya turned it towards her and looked at it.

Marlene had two adult daughters and a handsome husband. She grinned. One of the girls looked like her mom, and one looked like her dad.

Whose picture was she going to put on the desk?

Certainly not her family. Gwen was a traitor, Kavina was

a miserable whinger, and Lorenzo was never around. Hence, it had to be one with her and her dad. Her graduation was a more recent one.

Marlene came back into the office with effusive apologies. "Kiya, you will love working here," Marlene said. "I would not be leaving if it wasn't necessary, I can tell you that. We have a good staff, and we also have a nice comradery here."

"Why are you leaving?" Kiya asked.

"My husband and I are Bajan. Can't you tell by the accent?"

Kiya shook her head. "No, it's barely there."

"That means we've been here too long," Marlene chuckled. "We're going back home. We want to be near our grandkids.

"Oh," Kiya nodded, "okay."

"I have been hinting about leaving to Guy for a year now, and now finally, I have to go," Marlene said. "We need to be closer to my husband's parents too; they are not doing too well health-wise. It's just the perfect storm. I'll miss this place.

"Most of our operations are computerized, and the line staff is well trained. We share human resource services with the Wiley group, so payroll and all of that is taken care of.

"You will just need to run the store and manage the people. You will be fine."

Kiya nodded. She said it so many times it must be true.

Marlene took her on a slow tour of the place. She explained so many things Kiya had to take out a notebook eventually. When it was lunchtime, Marlene suggested going to the Yum Yum Cafe.

"I eat there most days," Marlene said. "The meals are tasty, and you get management vouchers for the month."

"Noted." Kiya nodded.

While they were on their way to Yum Yum, Kiya was

looking around, making a mental note to visit the shops she saw.

"Am I too late for lunch?" Lucia asked behind them.

Kiya spun around, and when she saw Lucia's dear face, she whooped in delight. It was not a managerial sound or reaction, but she didn't care who saw her and thought she was unprofessional.

Lucia greeted her just as excitedly. "Kiya gorgeous. I came by to find out how you were doing."

"I am fine so far. This place is lovely," Kiya said. "I can't believe how nice it is. And it's huge and busy, and the farm store is not what I imagined a farm store would be like."

Lucia grinned. "I'll take it from here, Marlene."

Marlene smiled at the two of them, "I understand, we have more lunchtimes Kiya."

"Are you starving?" Lucia asked after Marlene walked ahead. "We could take a Wiley Complex tour."

"I'm not hungry," Kiya said, "that would be very nice. I have been hankering to see inside some of these stores."

Lucia grinned. "You'll get used to it. I thought the same when I just came here, but now I'm all blasé about it? How are you settling in with your father's friends?"

"I had to move," Kiya said. "It was too cramped and crowded, and I couldn't sleep."

"So, where are you now?" Lucia asked, alarmed.

"I got a place to stay with one, Janet Forbes. Ace Jackson's aunt."

"Ace Jackson?" Lucia grinned. "I know Ace Jackson pretty well. How is he these days?"

"He's gorgeous," Kiya said dreamily. "Tall, dark and handsome doesn't begin to describe him."

Lucia laughed. "I know, I know. There was a time when my mother was pushing me to marry him."

"He told me that you guys almost had a relationship," Kiya said jealously.

Lucia looked at her and laughed. "I hope you are not feeling jealous. There is nobody for me but Guy. But Ace is a very lovely gentleman. I can't believe he hasn't married yet. He's a sweet and caring person."

Lucia looked at Kiya knowingly. "You two wouldn't make a lovely couple. Are you over Sylvester, yet?"

"I have been over, Sylvester," Kiya snorted. "It's my sister that I still can't stand. The betrayal is real. She is family, he was just a horny man in lust, and she is my relative who I thought I could at least trust."

"You'll work it out with her eventually," Lucia said easily. "Time has a way of taking care of these situations. One day, you'll wake up in the morning, and you can't remember what the bad feeling was about."

Kiya snorted. "I am going to need years."

"Years, decades," Lucia grinned. "It will fade."

They passed a clothing store with the logo Island Girl on the glass. There were some very fancy pieces on display. Kiya faltered in front of the display.

"That's Lyla's place. Her name means Island girl." Lucia said, "she has some nice clothes in there, doesn't she?"

"Lyla is one of your sisters-in-law?" Kiya asked.

"Yes," Lucia nodded. "She is Case Wiley's wife. She's from Cuba. She opened this place last year. She has a nice selection of clothing. Say how are you with clothes?"

"I bought two pants before I came here, a black one and a khaki one, and I'm going to wear them with some white tops until I can afford to do a bit of shopping."

Lucia shook her head. "No, we can't have that. As the head patron of the Farm Help Society, I think we should buy you a new wardrobe."

Kiya gasped. "Wardrobe, as in, more than one piece?"

"Oh yes! Lucia said excitedly. "I can see it now. We need to get you some nice church outfits, some nice work outfits, some nice night outfits... Ah, we have to get you the works... Some lovely date night outfits..."

"Date night!" Kiya exclaimed.

"Oh yes, we need to get you kitted out to get noticed by Ace."

"He already notices me," Kiya protested. "He dropped me to work today. He's inviting me to a charity concert later. His father said he likes me."

Lucia clapped her hands in glee. "Okay! I like that, one hurdle down, but if we're going to do this makeover, we have to do this right. Not that you need much of a makeover, but we're going to have to rub off some of the country and put on some sophistication."

They entered Island Girl clothing, and Lucia greeted the girl at the front by name.

"Amanda. This is a very dear friend of mine, and she needs everything,"

Kiya murmured uncomfortably. "Lucia! I can't accept this. This is too much!"

"You can, and you will accept this. This is a gift. You are a friend. You deserve a break. Don't argue. After this, we should do our nails and hair. I'm glad you're in Kingston. I finally have a girlfriend I can do stuff with. All of my sisters-in-law are super busy, overachievers."

"I have to get back to work," Kiya protested.

"You have two weeks with Marlene and just one night to wow everybody at this charity concert at Ace's church. And if Ace is not the one for you, trust me, there are a lot of lovely men at that church. You need to look fine, as in stop-traffic-fine."

"Don't you have anything better to do?" Kiya mumbled ungratefully.

"Oh yes, I do. I have my kid and my brother's kid at home, but I think I need some adult activity, and this is fun."

"Which one of your brothers has a kid?" Kiya asked.

"Earl." Lucia grimaced. "Remember Nova, who had that pregnancy that she tried to pass off as Guy's?"

Kiya nodded. "The entire community knows about that incident."

"Well, Nova was pregnant for Earl, and she had a pretty little girl she named Crystal. They almost didn't need to do a DNA test; the child is the spitting image of my mother."

"Imagine that," Kiya whistled, "so how is it that you are taking care of her?"

"Nova is working in Cayman, and she left her daughter with Earl. Earl left Crystal with my mother, who is getting married soon and does not want any child-rearing responsibilities, so I was the next logical choice. I don't mind, though. She is an adorable child."

"So you have a four-year-old and a two-year-old at home," Kiya asked, "what do you do when you travel?"

"Leave them with Guy and the nanny." Lucia giggled, "he surprisingly doesn't mind. Enough about me, I am so looking forward to getting you all dressed up and sophisticated looking. Please don't deny me this small pleasure."

Kiya chuckled. "Okay. Far be it from me to stop my rich friends from doing stuff for me."

"That's the spirit," Lucia said. "I wonder if you can come up to the farm soon. I'll be going to New York for two weeks for another exhibition, but I'll be back, and then you'll have to visit, and we can have some fun."

Chapter Seven

Ace was in between patients when his father appeared at the door, a big grin on his face.

"Ace Jackson Jr., you have my blessing to go forward with Kiya Brady."

"I wasn't aware that I asked for your blessing, or that it was even an issue."

Ace Sr. chuckled. "Getting your parents' blessing is important in some cultures. Anyway, I am happy that she's the woman who has your interest.

"She's George Brady's girl. George is a good sort, an upstanding man, a humanitarian, and I know he grew his children with his values."

Ace cleared his throat. "Quite résumé there for George."

"And it helps that his daughter is pretty and has an engaging personality," Ace Sr. chuckled. "I see grandchildren in my future. Ace the third, and Alice, the first. We need some girls in our family."

"Dad, don't you have anything better to do?"

"Oh, I do," Ace Sr. winked at him. "but getting rid of your single state is far more important to me right now. Tell me honestly, do you like her?"

"Yes, I do," Ace said, "As a matter of fact, I was just thinking about her. I know already that you like her. You told her that story about your mother, and the fact that we're fake Jackson's."

"A girl needs to know the type of family she's getting involved with," Ace Sr. chuckled.

"You are moving too fast." Ace shook his head. "Too, too fast."

"Your mother and I got married after six weeks." Ace Sr. fanned him off. "Forty years later, here we are. Say, I'm going to invite Kiya to our anniversary party."

"You just met her," Ace said.

"And I like her, so I'm going to invite her tonight. She should see that your old dad celebrates forty years of marriage and that you have a good example to follow."

"Dad, I have a patient in ten minutes. I have no time for romance and all that it entails now."

"Your next patient is that Yara Carr girl." Ace Sr. scoffed. "I saw it on the schedule. There is nothing wrong with her. You should send her to Dr. Joy."

"The psychiatrist?" Ace chuckled. "Maybe one day, something will be wrong with her. She said she's having cluster headaches."

"No doubt caused by her single-minded determination to see you regularly." Ace Sr. chuckled. "I don't want her in our family, Ace. I want that girl, Kiya."

His father left the office, and Ace took a phone call from one of his more problematic patients, and then Yara came in.

"Two weddings, Ace Jr.," Yara said before she sat down.

"Two weddings and not even a dance with you? I expected you to ask me to dance with you at Tiana's wedding, but you didn't. Elsa's wedding was a hyped-up affair, and even the oldest of the old was on the dance floor, and you didn't ask me to dance. Is it that you can't dance?"

"Do you have an ailment I can help you with today, Yara?" Ace asked, subsiding in his chair. Yara was a pretty girl, stunning, actually. But there was no chemistry between them, much to his mother's chagrin.

She wouldn't mind if he dated Yara Carr and got married to her and had their families inextricably linked.

"I have a headache since Mason tied the knot with Elsa," Yara said, bemoaning her fate. "I want to know what's wrong with me. I am single, I am good looking. Before you accuse me of blowing my own horn, I have no time for false modesty. I know I look good. Mason bypassed me, and I just can't get through to you. Probably you should prescribe me some medication on how to get through to Ace Jr."

Ace steepled his fingers together. "Do you know the Bible text, 'They that wait upon the Lord shall renew their strength. They shall mount up with wings like eagles...'"

"If I wait, I'll be an old lady before anything happens, I saw this cartoon of an old lady at her honeymoon when she opened her legs bats flew out." Yara snorted. "I don't want bats and cobwebs to be under there for my honeymoon."

Ace laughed out loud. "You say the weirdest things."

"Do you know the text when the children of Israel were at the Red Sea? And the Lord said, 'Moses, what's in your hand?'"

Ace chuckled. "And Moses stretched out his rod?"

"Exactly." Yara nodded. "There's a time to wait and the time for action. There is a time to use what you have in hand. You know what, I'm going to stop beating around the bush, I am asking you out on a date, and you can't say no, Ace. Don't disappoint me."

Ace held up his hand. "Okay, a date it is."

Yara smiled. "You see, sometimes the Lord just wants us to use what is in our hands. I'll call you and tell you when and where."

****

Ace drove into the Wiley complex and stopped in front of the farm store. He wasn't prompt. It was fifteen minutes after five. He hoped Kiya wasn't waiting for him too long. He picked up the phone to call her, and then a familiar-looking girl stepped outside the store.

Familiar because that could not be Kiya. When he had picked her up this morning, she was in black pants and a white shirt. Her hair slicked back in a bun. The girl he was looking at now seemed unfamiliar. Her hair was out and curly, in a fluffy style. She was wearing a wrap dress that emphasized her shape and matching shoes in a taupe color. Her lips were glistening red.

"What on earth!" Ace actually thought that Kiya had a twin sister. He didn't realize his mouth was opened until Kiya started laughing.

"You should see yourself," Kiya said, opening the car door and getting in. "You look shocked."

"And you look different," Ace said. "Like wow, different."

"Thank you." Kiya smiled. "I have some packages to put in the car. Can we take them, do you think?"

"Packages? Sure," Ace said slowly. "Well, they're more like suitcases." Kiya grinned. " I went shopping today. My friend Lucia took me out."

"Lucia Wiley?" Ace asked.

"That Lucia, she thought I needed some things," Kiya shook her head, "but it ended up being a whole wardrobe. I have more things than I've ever had in my entire life. Could you help?"

She got out of the car, and Ace followed, watching as this strange, beautiful creature walked before him, more confident than she had seemed in the morning.

"Lucia said I need to get the country-sheen off of me." She turned, her hair following in a cloud of curls. "She made me go to the hairdresser. Apparently, this style is what they call a wash-and-go. Can you believe it? All I need to do is wet it up, put some gel in it, and I have curls. I didn't even know I had curls."

Ace chuckled. "Okay."

The store was closed for the day, but the security guard let Kiya back in. There were four brand new traveling suitcases at the front.

Ace rounded his eyes. "What!"

"Lucia said it would make her feel better if she went on a mad shopping spree with me," Kiya said. "I couldn't help it. I had to make my friend feel better."

Ace wheeled the bags to the car and picked them up, they were heavy.

"One of them only has shoes," Kiya said almost apologetically. "She even says she has more at her house, and I need to help her out with them."

After Ace put the bags in the car, he turned to Kiya. "Is that all?"

"She made me buy two new handbags. Let me go and get them," Kiya said excitedly. "Today actually feels like Christmas."

She ran inside, got her two handbags, and then came and sat inside the vehicle on the passenger side.

"Now, today was fun." She grinned. "Oh, I had such mad fun. I didn't know how much fun you could have shopping. And I had no idea how many things I needed."

Ace smiled. "Did you get any work done?"

"In the morning I did, but it was all shopping in the afternoon. Marlene, that's the outgoing manager, she said she understood I needed to get some things. Marlene probably thought I was going to get an outfit or two for work, I had no idea I would be getting a whole wardrobe" Kiya mused. "Lucia has this way of making you feel as if you're doing her a favor. I didn't feel like a charity case at all. When I protested, she said that my father used to give them food when she was poor, down and out."

"Yes, George has a reputation for that in the community." Ace nodded. "You are reaping your father's good deeds."

"Amen," Kiya said contemplatively. "When I have some means, I'm going to share it, just like Lucia."

"Pay it forward," Ace nodded. "That's a good motto."

"Did you get the chance to practice?" Kiya asked.

"Only for about an hour," Ace said. "I can't believe that we're going to sing without practicing with each other. We have never done that before. We'll have to steal some moments before the show begins, but Trey is running late as usual, and Deuce had an emergency. Maybe I'll have to do a solo, who knows. In that case, I'll just do my signature song, *I've Got Friends in High Places*."

"Love that song," Kiya said. "I believe it. I feel it to my bones. I've got friends in high places, and I'm going to be with them one day. Love it."

Ace watched her expression and smiled.

Was she really as sweet as she seemed? Maybe he should find out if she had any quirks before he liked her even more than he did now and save himself the heartache.

But her charms or lack thereof were not the only thing in contention for his affection.

She could be his sister. That thought was never far from his mind. Janet had really done a number on him.

Chapter Eight

It wasn't long before they drove into the church's parking lot, people were there already, he recognized quite a few of the choir members' cars. He parked at the same time that Solomon, the choir director, parked.

"Now, this is a big parking lot," Kiya said. "I made a note to myself to stop exclaiming about how big everything was and how different everything was. But man, this is huge. Lucia said I'd get used to it."

"You have never left Portland?" Ace turned to her. "Never in all your life?

Kiya shook her head. "Just once, it was to a church function in Kingston. My dad kept a tight rein on me, I think more than he did the others. He has this theory that I look like my mom, and he feared I would leave like her.

"I don't know what his reasoning was. So he kept tight reins on me, tighter than he did with my other siblings, and I accepted it because I am the obedient daughter. So here I am twenty-six years old and not well-traveled even in my own country."

"I am going to have to show you everywhere in Kingston," Ace said. "Clear your schedule for a nightly tour. That is when I'll be free."

"Okay." Kiya smiled. "I'm fine with that."

"Come on, let's go," Ace said.

They got out of the car.

Solomon looked across at Ace. "Hey, Ace! What's up, man? I might have to do a solo. Trey and Deuce are nowhere to be found."

"No sweat," Solomon said. "We have your back. We have two items on the program... Who is that?"

He looked around Ace and widened his eyes when he saw Kiya. "Wow. Whoo-hoo."

"This is Kiya Brady, my friend," Ace said.

"And I am Solomon King, his choir director. Are you single... I meant, can you sing?"

Kiya laughed. "I am single, and I can sing."

"And are you going to be visiting us for the next couple of months?" Solomon asked.

"Sure, why not?" Kiya nodded. "I like this parking lot already."

"Oh, the people here are wonderful," Solomon got into his greeting mode. "We are friendly, and we are kind, and we are the best thing that has ever happened to you."

"Overkill, Solomon." Ace chuckled. "Overkill."

"When pretty girls darken our door," Solomon said, "we have to keep them, especially pretty girls who can sing. Do you want to try out tonight, Kiya?"

Kiya nodded. "Sure. I was the head of my praise team back home."

"What!" Solomon chuckled. "Well okay, then. Come

along."

She looked at Ace. "Should I?"

Ace nodded. "Go ahead. I'm going to call my brothers to see where they are."

Kiya followed Solomon to the main edifice. There were two buildings on the huge plot of land. One seemed like the church hall or a mini church, and the next was the major church. People were already in there practicing.

"What time is this concert?" She asked Solomon.

"Seven," Solomon said. "And then the party will begin. Listen up people," he said when he entered the main sanctuary, "The king is here."

Quite a few persons who are milling around looked up and waved.

"What do you say to your king?"

"I say," one tall, pretty girl said, "what took you so long? You told us to be here at five-thirty, it is now quarter to six. Do you think we have time to waste, King Solomon?"

"That's Yara," Solomon said under his breath. "Yara Carr has no respect for the king. Watch out for her; she's after Ace."

Kiya opened their mouth. "But Ace and I are just..."

"Friends?" Solomon chuckled. "Hmm...okay, everyone, let's get into formation."

Without much prompting, what seemed like a huge choir started gathering on the platform. "I see you all took my punctuality conversation to heart."

"More like dictation," Yara said.

Kiya followed closely behind Solomon.

"Everybody, this is Kiya Brady. She is coming from the lovely parish of Portland, where the seas are blue, the trees are green and lush, and the girls are gorgeous."

There were quite a few chuckles.

"And she says she can sing. She will be making her debut so that we can hear what she's capable of, and then we'll ask her to join our award-winning choir. Which houses the magnificent, Case Wiley."

Kiya smiled. Solomon was obviously dramatic.

"He will be doing a solo tonight, and we will be backing him on the song 'God and Life'. Do you know it, Kiya?" He turned to her.

Kiya nodded. "I do. I know all the songs on Case Wiley's album."

"A gospel-loving fan, praise the Lord!" Solomon said snarkily, "this lot are not into gospel music much and they are a church choir!"

His choir was obviously used to him and his antics. They waited patiently while he came to the front. "Do you know the song; *I'm No Longer Slave to Fear*?"

"Oh yes," Kiya nodded. "I do. That was one of our staple songs back at my church."

"Lead out." Solomon handed her the microphone.

"I should just sing?" Kiya said nervously. There were thirty persons behind her, waiting to hear.

"That's usually the best way to do it," Solomon said. "Just go for it."

She took the mic, adrenaline flowing through her. The people on the instruments were waiting.

"Am I going to get some music with this?" she asked.

"Cocky!" Solomon grinned. "I like that. This sounds like you know what you're going to do?"

Kiya said nervously. "I think I know what I am doing."

"Just go along, sing, let us hear what you have, and then I'll tell the musicians when to come in," Solomon said.

Kiya started singing. *"You unravel me with a melody... I am no longer a slave to fear,"* Her voice rung out deep and strong and sweet in the empty church.

Solomon had a pleased look on his face. He nodded to the musicians, and they started playing the hook, and then the choir joined in.

"You are a natural," Solomon said when she was done, "and yes, you can join us when the program begins. We would love to have you."

"You mean participate?"

"Yes, we'll be doing a praise and worship segment," Solomon said as if it was a major privilege. "We are an award-winning choir, did I say?"

"Several times." Kiya chuckled.

She was introduced around after their one-hour practice and was waylaid by none other than Yara, who introduced herself as Yara Carr.

Her brother Cole Carr had shaken her hand a little bit too long. He was cute. Most of the men in the choir were good looking.

Yara pulled her aside. "Where did Solomon find you?"

"Oh, I came with Ace," Kiya said.

"Junior or Senior," Yara asked interestedly.

"Junior," Kiya replied.

"I am on the verge of making him my boyfriend. So you need to back off. Just a friendly warning," Yara said.

"On the verge, it's not really happening, is it?" Kiya said impishly.

"I thought you were a mousy country girl," Yara sighed, "you are going to be trouble for me, I can feel it."

"Yara, leave my friend alone," Solomon said, pulling Kiya away. "I have a feeling she will be my lead singer in the second soprano section."

"She does sound good," Yara said grudgingly. "I wished she sounded otherwise, but oh well."

"Told you to watch out for her, but she gives credit where it's due," Solomon grinned. "But it's all good. We're all lovely Christian people. We love the Lord, and there will be no fighting, especially over Ace Jackson. I run a cohesive outfit. My choir is united. She will just have to learn how to get along with you."

Kiya nodded. "Okay, then."

****

It was an interesting program that was filled with music and laughter. There was a comedy section where a standup comedian gave some hilarious jokes.

Kiya couldn't remember having such a good time in all her twenty-six years on the planet. She laughed until she was hoarse as the comedian imitated the different types of people in the church.

She sat with the choir in the loft, beside a girl named Susan, who couldn't stop talking about Cole, Yara's brother.

"We're engaged," Susan said.

Kiya nodded. "Well, congratulations. I wish you all the best. I was engaged for five years, and nothing happened, he got married to my sister instead."

Susan frowned. "Well, I'm going to make sure something happens. He is not getting away from me."

At the end of the program, Kiya ended up finding Ace, who had eventually sung with his brothers.

They sounded good. They sounded as if they had practiced all day and night, instead of a quick session in the parking lot. They harmonized well.

Kiya had not gotten the chance to see them close up, but when she did, she was awestruck. Deuce or DJ, she corrected herself mentally, looked very much like Ace. The three brothers were tall. Trey was light-skinned and wore a goatee; he looked a lot different than Ace or DJ.

Ace saw her hovering in the crowd and called her over, introducing her to his brothers. They greeted her, but in the crush of people, they spoke briefly. Ace Sr. found them and was jovial as usual.

"How do you like our church?" He asked. "I see they already roped you into the choir."

"I love it," Kiya said, "I can't wait to come back here."

"Atta girl," Ace Sr. patted her on the shoulder good-naturedly. "That's what I love to hear."

Celia Jackson was a little behind her husband and looking cross.

"Mom, this is Kiya," Ace said, introducing his mother to her. "Kiya, this is Celia Jackson, my mother."

Celia looked Kiya over, searching her features before she actually exclaimed. "You look just like Charlotte! I see why Norman here is excited about meeting you. Your mother had that effect on men."

She said it as if she had a bad taste in her mouth.

"Mom," Ace frowned. "What are you doing?"

"Just making a general observation." Celia gritted out. "She looks like her mother. Do you know how your mother used to be?"

"Mom!"

"Celia!"

The two Aces said, almost at the same time.

Kiya recoiled. She could see venom, hatred, and anger blazing from Celia Jackson's eyes. What had she done to this woman? She had never met her before.

They left shortly after that the crush of the crowd around made it almost impossible to communicate easily, and Kiya was happy for that. The one brush with Celia Jackson had her shaken.

Kiya was silent on the way back, a far cry from when she had arrived at the church. Ace was contemplative too.

"Why is your mother so hostile?" she asked.

"She's not usually like that."

"Your dad is nice, but your mom," Kiya made a face, "I don't think I want to ever see her again."

"That's a pity," Ace said, "because my dad wanted to invite you to their fortieth wedding anniversary."

"I think I'll take a pass," Kiya said.

"He'll convince you," Ace murmured. "And don't worry about my mom. The next time you meet her, she will not be like this, I am going to have a chat with her."

There was a certainty and a threat in his tone.

Chapter Nine

Ace got up and looked at the clock groggily. He had to go to Sunday dinner at his parent's house. He could do with a sleep-in. He hadn't slept for most of the night. An emergency with one of his patients had him up really late, but it was a weekly Sunday dinner tradition with the Jackson family. Barring death or surgery, he had to show up.

His mother insisted on that family time. They all lived in the same town. It was only logical to meet up regularly.

He swiped his hand across his face. He lived to the closest to his parents. As a matter of fact, he was just two streets from their house. It took him five minutes to walk over. He was privileged to live in the prestigious neighborhood, in a four-bedroom house with a spacious yard that was filled with fruit trees.

It had been his granduncle Tobias' place, and when he died, Ace had inherited it.

Over the years, he had done several upgrades to drag the

place into the 21st century. He pulled the curtains and looked out at his backyard. As usual, his lawn was immaculately done, his mango tree was loaded with mangoes, and it was a bright, sunshiny day.

He should be feeling enthusiastic about going over to his parents, but he was bone tired. He had a quick shower, pulled on his walking shoes, shaved, brushed his teeth, and inspected his bloodshot eyes and headed to the door.

It was a pleasant walk in the neighborhood. He passed Mrs. Clover's garden. She had a long running competition with his mother to see whose garden looked the best. Their gardens were opposite each other in a cul-de-sac. It was the prettiest part of Maple Drive. He looked from one to the other and smiled.

Mrs. Clover had white hydrangeas. His mother would have white hydrangeas soon. Quade was standing in the driveway and looking around when he got there.

"I am always amazed at what a green thumb, Aunt Celia has," Quade said, shaking his head. "Everything here is so lush and pretty. I could stand here all day."

Ace chuckled. "I thought they worked on your garden as well."

"Yes, they do, but it's not like this. Aunt Celia always preserves the best for herself because of her plant war with Mrs. Clover."

"So, how is it going?" Ace asked.

Quade was his business partner in a venture called Golden Acres. It was a retirement community that they ran together. Not only were they business partners and cousins, but they were friends.

After his parents died, Quade had lived with them for a while. And then his grand-uncle Tobias and grand aunt Florence had taken him to live with them in the States.

Quade was an honorary brother.

"How is what going? Quade asked. "Our joint business venture is running smoothly. Our new entertainment coordinator is causing quite a little stir, though."

"Why, isn't she working out well?" Ace asked.

"Oh, yes, she is," Quade joked. "She's working out a little too well. She has all the old men vying for her attention and she is a hit with the ladies because she has them going on tours to different sections of the island, making them revisit their childhood places."

Ace laughed. "That's clever."

"What are you two laughing about in the middle of the driveway?" Deuce asked, coming from the side of the house.

"We have a new employee that's causing quite a stir," Ace said. "A classic case of a pretty girl and lusty old men."

Quade shook his head. "May I not be that thirsty when I'm old."

"Pretty girl, huh?" Deuce shook his head. "Maybe I should take a visit to see this pretty girl. I haven't been up to your place in quite a long time."

"Understandable," Quade said. "Your specialty is pediatrics, we are geriatrics."

"That's no excuse, but I have to say since I have been filling in for David who is gone on a sabbatical for six months, I appreciate how hectic this profession is."

"David on a sabbatical?" Quade raised his eyebrows. "I thought you were filling in for him for a couple of weeks, not six months."

"His doctor ordered him to rest, he was burnt out." Deuce shook his head. "Now that I am filling in for him, I can see why. The workload at the hospital is off the chains crazy."

"Which means no social life," Quade grinned. "Your dad is not going to like that, DJ."

"It's not for long," Deuce said tiredly. "When David comes back, I can go back to private practice. Hey Ace, do you guys miss me over at the complex?"

Ace chuckled. "Not really,"

Deuce made a face. "And there was thinking I was the life of the party."

"Guys come this way," Ace Sr. called out. "Trey said he had surgery, so he's not coming, and I'm getting hungry. Your mother is about to serve hors d'oeuvres."

They all trooped onto the back patio. That is where they usually had dinner, whether rain or shine. His mother had transformed around there into a different world. She had a waterfall surrounded by flowers. It was an unexpected oasis that had a wow factor on guests.

"So, what were you all whispering about?" Ace Sr. asked jovially. "Is it Ace's new girlfriend?"

"Ace has a new girlfriend?" Deuce raised his eyebrow.

"That girl from Thursday. The one with the voice and pretty face." Ace Sr. chuckled. "It reminds me of the time I met one, Celia Walker. She also had a voice on her, and she was pretty as a picture, still is actually."

His mother joined them on the patio with a platter filled with hors d'oeuvres. His father slapped her on her butt playfully, and she giggled.

"You know, she used to act like she was hard to get?" Ace Sr. said, "but when I first saw her, I said, 'this girl is not going to slip through my fingers'. Of course, I was just a country doctor, and she belonged to the prestigious Sunny Ray and the Hurricanes band. I was a nobody to her fame."

Celia laughed. "I wouldn't call our little home-grown band prestigious. Besides, Janet had her eye on Norman, and I didn't want to come between true love."

Ace Sr. laughed. "You had your eye on Micky Wiley. It

still baffles me as to why."

Celia looked at Ace guiltily. "Come on, eat up. You have the hors d'oeuvres. It should whet your appetite for what's coming. I did mutton, and I have baked chicken, done just the way you want it. I should go get the drinks."

Ace offered to help. "I'll help you, Mom."

He wanted to talk to her privately anyway. He didn't like how she treated Kiya at the charity concert. And it was obvious when Micky Wiley's name was mentioned she started getting jumpy.

Celia slumped her shoulders. He was the last person she wanted to help from. She knew he was about to give her a stern talking to, and she didn't want to deal with that now.

The kitchen was newly renovated. His mother had shiny new appliances all over, and a fridge that showed what was inside when the glass door was tapped. It was a state-of-the-art kitchen. It was the first time Ace was seeing the finished product. He looked around. "This is nice."

"Thank you," Celia said.

"Can we talk about the other night and your attitude, Mom?"

Celia frowned at him. "I don't want to talk about it."

"You were quite rude to Kiya."

"I wasn't rude, I was pleasant," she paused, because it was an obvious lie, "well… pleasant enough."

"That's not true," Ace narrowed his eyes at her. "Why are you acting so strangely? You gave me your blessing to see Kiya. You said there was no reason I shouldn't."

"And I meant it," Celia growled, "but there is Yara Carr. Why aren't you interested in Yara? Why are you taking this girl around and introducing her to everyone and making Yara jealous?"

"Yara? Ace frowned. "How did Yara come into this?"

"Yara likes you. She is from the Carr family. Do I have to spell it out?"

"You are not a snob, and in case you have forgotten, people don't go choosing people because of which family they belong to. I've never really cared about that sort of thing, and I didn't know you cared either."

"I am friends with her mother," Celia said, "And Yara said she wants to be your friend, and now this girl, Kiya, comes from the belly of the country and is taking over."

"She's not taking over. Where did you get that idea from, and why were you so jumpy when Dad spoke about you having an eye on Micky Wiley? Do you still love Micky Wiley, Mom?"

"Who said I love him in the first place!" Celia growled. "What's the matter with you, Ace? This is not a topic that I want to talk about!"

"Is he my father?" Ace asked forcefully.

Celia glared at him. "Keep your voice down, and no to all your questions. It's ridiculous, this stupid conclusion that you've drawn about Micky Wiley. He is not your father. I repeat, he is not your father. Ace Sr. is your father. And if I'm to be honest, the reason why I don't like Kiya is because she is not from good stock."

Ace laughed loudly. "What do you mean not from good stock? She's not an animal."

"Her mother, Charlotte, was, how should I say it delicately? Not faithful to her husband."

"Have you ever been unfaithful to yours?" Ace threw the criticism back at her.

"We're not talking about me," Celia gritted out. "You asked me why I was rude to Kiya, your precious Kiya. She is pretty, but she might be just like her mom. As a matter of fact, she looks too much like that woman."

"Were you always faithful to Dad?" Ace asked.

Celia turned her back to him and started gathering glasses from the cabinet. "I don't appreciate being asked these kinds of questions, Ace, and from my son at that."

"Pardon me, Mom, but you sound a tad bit defensive."

"Of course, I'm defensive. My honor is being questioned."

"And yet you do not answer the question?" Ace stressed.

"Have you asked Ace Sr. if he has been faithful to me?"

"Why would I?" Ace asked. "Men don't have children, and when paternity matters are at stake, it's the woman that we have to ask about faithfulness, not the man."

"There are no paternity questions at stake," Celia gritted out. "And my faithfulness or lack thereof was not the topic of conversation. We were talking about the fact that Kiya's mother was not the best person."

"And she died when Kiya was young," Ace said. "And had no influence on her upbringing. By all accounts, she only had her dad, and he was as strict as possible."

"Do you know how she died?" Celia asked. "She ran off again, to be with Micky Wiley, and then got pregnant again. She left her four children and husband behind and went into premature labor and died in childbirth.

"Now tell me, how can a sick woman be going back to the same old man, over and over again, getting pregnant for him, over and over again, leaving her husband and her children? They're not even his."

Ace sighed. "Your fury for a dead woman's deeds is admirable. I'm pretty sure that you will get brownie points in heaven for your righteous indignation, but you have not answered my question. I cannot help but think that you are very upset about the fact that this Charlotte lady kept going to Micky Wiley. You have a thing for Micky Wiley, and even Dad knows. Do you think Kiya is Micky's daughter?"

"Do I think... why do you think everybody is Micky's child?" Celia blurted out. "It's as if you're obsessed with Micky Wiley. I don't know if she is, but I know that you are not his child. Now have some pity on me, and stop asking me these stupid questions, Ace."

She put the ice in the glasses a little too forcefully and then handed him the drinks.

"I'm behind you with the glasses," she clipped. Ace didn't want his mother to be mad at him. He hated it when she was. He was on the verge of apologizing, but then he changed his mind. Why should he be apologizing for wanting to know the truth?

"And the truth will set you free," he murmured under his breath.

Celia glared at him.

She served the drinks and stonily and sat across from them.

"What did you do to Mom?" Deuce asked.

"I merely asked her why she was so rude to Kiya the other night, and she blasted me," Ace replied.

"I wasn't rude to the girl," Celia said.

"She seems nice," Deuce grinned. "I liked her, Ace."

"And I like her too," Ace Sr. chuckled. "And I'm hoping that Ace won't let this one fall through his fingers. Celia will come around. Kiya is George's daughter, she has good genes running through her blood."

Ace looked at his mother's reaction, she turned away from him.

"You know who else has good genes, Yara Carr," Celia said smugly. "That's what I told Ace just now."

"You love who you love." Ace took a sip of his drink. "You're attracted to who you're attracted to."

"That's right," Ace Sr. said. "That has always been the case for the men in our family."

Am I biologically a part of this family? Ace asked his mother silently.

Celia met his unspoken query with a fulsome glare.

****

Kiya spent her morning arranging her new clothes and singing gospel songs at the top of her voice. She had woken up feeling good. She felt contented and happy. She hadn't felt this way in a long time. Not since Sylvester and Gwen, and even now the thought of them didn't seem to have any effect on her. She hadn't been gone long, and the thought of them had no power to hurt her anymore. That was what a little distance from a situation did to a person.

That was probably why she felt generous enough to call her sister. She hadn't told Gwen that she was leaving Portland, and at one time, they had been close. Gwen couldn't help it that she was pretty, or help the fact that Sylvester fell in love with her. Yes, she could have refused to sleep with him behind her back, but she was not in the mood for darker thoughts.

Kiya waited for her cellphone to ring, and when Gwen answered, she was grumpy.

"So, you called me to gloat?" Gwen said.

"Huh?" Kiya asked, puzzled.

"I am sure Daddy or Kavina, who loves misery, called you to let you know that Sylvester left."

"Sylvester left?" Kiya gripped the phone closer to her ears. "When? You guys just got married!"

"He doesn't know his mind." Gwen snarled. "He's a wishy-washy fool that moved back in with his parents, claiming that I nagged him too much. He said he made a mistake in marrying me."

Gwen started crying. "The idiot said I had serious issues that are above his pay grade. All I have been doing is pushing him about fixing up the dilapidated house he is supposed to fix up for us to move in. I want to move out of here. Daddy is not as accommodating as he once was. And you know what the idiot said?"

"What did he say?" Kiya murmured.

"He said, I have no concept of the real world, and he has to have a plan and money, blah blah, blah. I thought he had the money and a plan for it already. How was I to know that he didn't?"

"Hmm." Kiya looked in the ceiling, trying not to smile.

She had been saving to help with the repairs for the house and budgeting. They had a plan. A plan that she had commissioned an architect to do for them. When Sylvester married Gwen, she had torn up the plan, she had also given him back his money, which hadn't been much, she was the one who had been saving religiously.

She couldn't laugh at her sister's pain. No, she wouldn't. That would not be Christian-like, and besides, her father had spent a good chunk of money on that wedding.

"You guys have to work it out," Kiya said soothingly to her bawling sister. She couldn't believe she was saying this. "You two really didn't know each other before you tied the knot, did you? It's just growing pains."

"He said he's not sure that he loves me." Gwen hiccupped. "He said he was just filled with lust, and now he is paying for it because I am high maintenance."

Gwen wailed for a good two minutes, and Kiya sat through it, wondering if she had enough credit on the phone to withstand the conversation.

She wondered where her sympathy was. She wanted to tell her sister, 'I told you so,' in the snarkiest voice possible.

"He said, I'm pretty and useless," Gwen choked out, "and that I how was the biggest mistake he has ever made. I have to get out of here. Can I come stay with you, Kiya?"

"Uhm." Kiya sat down hard on her settee. What was she to say? 'Suck it up, life is not all about flowers and chocolate?' Or, 'Hell no! I don't want you in my space right now.'

Instead, she said soothingly. "You can't leave. If you leave, you won't be able to work it out with Sylvester. This little phase will pass, and you two will be good again when you remember what brought you both together in the first place."

"It was just sex, and it's not even fun with him anymore." Gwen wailed. "You didn't miss anything when you didn't do it with him, trust me. You owe me, Kiya. I saved you from Sylvester."

Kiya thought of a way to extricate herself from the conversation, she didn't want to discuss Gwen and Sylvester's sex life.

And though Gwen had a point about saving her from Sylvester, it didn't have to go down that way. She would never fully trust her sister again.

While she was thinking exactly how to formulate her thoughts, a beep indicating another call sounded on her phone.

"I have to go now, Gwen," Kiya said. "There's another call coming in, but whatever you do, don't give up on your marriage."

She ended the call gratefully and responded to the next one.

The call was from an unknown number. Ace Sr.'s jovial voice came on the line.

"Kiya Brady, I hope you don't mind; Ace gave me your number."

"I don't mind," Kiya smiled. He was always so upbeat and

positive it was a treat hearing from him.

"Well, I'm sure I mentioned my anniversary to you before. It will be forty glorious years. Well, some of them were not so glorious, all marriages go through bad patches."

"Yes, you did mention it." Kiya thought of Celia's scowling face. She was almost sure that Celia was the cause of the bad patches.

"I am calling to personally invite you. Ace said you may be reluctant to come, so I had to call to let you know it would mean a lot to me if you showed up."

Kiya bit her lip. She didn't want to encounter Celia Jackson again. "I… er…"

"Please say you will come," Ace Sr. cajoled, "this year we are having a huge party, Celia even has a party planner. Usually, we have the anniversary party at home, but this year we're thinking of having it at the Carr's residence. Ace will take you. He knows where it is."

She couldn't say no, when he sounded so eager to have her there. Maybe her contact with Celia Jackson could be limited. It sounded as if it would be a large event.

"Okay, sir. Thank you for the invite," Kiya said.

Before Ace Sr. hung up the phone, she could swear she heard Celia Jackson's voice in the background yelling, "Norman, are you inviting people who are not on the list?"

The lady didn't like her, and Kiya was going to find out why.

Chapter Ten

Kiya, I thought of nothing all week but the anniversary party. What would she wear? It had to be fancy, obviously. She called Lucia and told her of her predicament, and by Tuesday, Lucia had shown up at her office. She had five dresses for her to choose from.

"Choose one," Lucia said. "Take it if you like it." Kiya liked a blue dress. It fit her perfectly. Which was fortunate because one morning, Ace mentioned that his favorite color was blue. He still picked her up every morning like clockwork. Kiya imagine that Janet was fuming, and she was right.

Wednesday, Janet called her to invite her to breakfast.

"And how was my nephew doing?" she asked as soon as Kiya sat down.

"He's fine," Kiya said. She could feel the curiosity rolling off Janet.

"That's nice to hear," Janet said snarkily. "Since I'm his patient and he has not come inside to say hello." Kiya smiled but didn't say a word.

"And I told you to stay away from him, and yet he's still picking you up."

"I have no other means of reaching work," Kiya said gently. "I checked the cost of the taxi service here, and it's expensive."

"You are dressing better these days," Janet said, "and you can't find taxi fare? Speak the truth. You are into my nephew."

"I do like him," Kiya said. "Ace is fun, and he's a nice guy. I don't understand. What is it with you and your sister?"

"My sister?" Janet asked. "What did my sister say?"

"She didn't say anything. She just acts weird. You both are acting weird. Why can't I talk to Ace? Why can't he pick me up? Why can't we have a relationship?"

"Because of the stupid country soap opera. That's why," Janet snorted. "And I can't tell you anything because it is top secret."

"So, I should just trust your word for it that I should stay away from Ace, and that's it?" Kiya asked.

"When you put it that way," Janet said. "Iit does sound weird. I'll need to ask my sister permission to tell you some things."

"What things?" Kiya was confused afresh.

"The things of the past, the things of your parents and their shenanigans, and all of that madness," Janet growled. "And I have no authority to go into all of that."

Kiya was still confused. She looked down at the toast and the eggs and wondered if Janet was slightly touched in the head and if her sister had a touch of it, too.

"What do you think about DJ?" Janet asked after a short silence.

Kiya frowned. "DJ, as in Ace's brother?"

"Yes, that same DJ," Janet said. "the one that looks like

Ace."

Kiya frowned. "He seems nice I met him the other night. He just said hello. I haven't really spoken to him or anything."

"Did you meet Trey," Janet asked.

Kiya nodded. "Yes, I did. I met Trey."

"Trey is single and available," Janet said. "Why don't you choose Trey? Tell you what. I'll invite over Trey. And then we'll have lunch together. What do you say?"

"So, you don't want me to see Ace or DJ, but Trey is fine?"

"Yes," Janet nodded, "very fine."

"I don't get it."

Janet sighed a long, drawn-out sigh. "That's okay. One day you will get it, and you will thank me that I cared enough to warn you."

She changed the subject after that cryptic statement. "I heard that Ace Sr. is planning to invite you to his anniversary party."

"He just did," Kiya said. "He is a nice man."

"He's a troublemaker," Janet growled. "I think he is pushing Celia's buttons. I think he is punishing her."

Kiya was more confused than anything, after that little conversation. She excused herself hurriedly, went to get her bag, and waited at the gate for Ace. She was feeling quite troubled.

"Your aunt said that I should date your brother Trey and that I am to leave you and your brother, DJ, alone," Kiya said to him as soon as she got into the car. "I don't get this. And then she said your father is pushing your mother's buttons, by inviting me to the anniversary. What is going on about?"

Ace looked at her tiredly. "I wish I knew, but I was up late again, and my family's little shenanigans, I cannot process right now. Are you ready for the party?"

"More than ready." Kiya smiled. "I got a nice dress from

Lucia."

"She seemed to have taken you under her wings," Ace said. "it's good that you have a friend who is looking out for you. Did I mention that you look lovely today? That khaki is your color."

Kiya smiled. "Apart from the tiredness around your eyes, you don't look bad yourself."

"Listen, I can't pick you up this evening," Ace murmured, "I have an appointment. Is it possible for you to get somebody else to do it?"

"Sure." Kiya nodded. "Is this a problem, picking me up? I never really asked."

"No, it's not a problem," Ace said readily. "I just have a new patient scheduled for that time."

"I'll ask Marlene to drop me home," Kiya said. "We've been getting on so well. I'm kind of sorry to see her go. Just one more week and she's gone, and I'll be on my own managing the store. I have to admit I'm looking forward to having the desk to myself. And the whole process is not hard at all. I was nervous for nothing."

When Kiya entered the store, one of the cashiers, the most outgoing one, her name was Andrea, who had come in at the same time, looked at Ace as he drove away and then at Kiya. "Is that your boyfriend, Miss?"

"He's a friend," Kiya said.

"I'd give him eleven out of ten." Andrea grinned. "It must be hard for you keeping him as a friend, men who look like that are not friend zone material."

Kiya silently agreed with her.

****

The Carr's mansion was something spectacular.

"It's a hotel," Kiya, whispered.

Ace chuckled. "No, it's not. It's just an ordinary house for seriously rich people. They hold events here all the time. My mom is friends with Naomi Carr, and she probably invited all of Kingston to this anniversary celebration."

"Forty years is a long time to be married," Kiya said. "I like that about them. My sister Gwen just got married the other day, and already her husband left her."

Ace looked at Kiya, "your ex jumped ship already?"

"Oh yes," Kiya nodded.

"He sounds fickle," Ace mused. "I once read somewhere that both of you can't want to leave the marriage at the same time. In my parent's case, I doubt my father has ever wanted to leave. He loves my mom."

Kiya sighed wistfully. "I want to have something like that for myself."

"You know, I've watched my parents all my life. And though they've lasted this long and are still together, I don't want what they have, I want something different. I'm not criticizing them. Obviously, they make what they have work. Still, I would like more of a partnership, especially when it comes to bringing up children and something along the lines of total trust and faithfulness."

Kiya looked at him sharply. "Did they have some sort of problem in their marriage?"

"Everybody has problems." Ace smiled. "I think it's naive to think that you would never have any, and everything will be smooth sailing."

"That's what I told my sister," Kiya said.

"Well then, that is good advice," Ace said. "Come on, let's go. I think we're a little late, and DJ, Trey and I are supposed to be doing an item at the top of the program."

It was a large crowd, indeed, when they went around to the

pool area.

Kiya went with Ace but lost him after he was pulled away by someone who wanted his opinion on something, but she wasn't alone for a long. Yara Carr found her in the crush of people.

"So he took you to his parents' anniversary party. Things are serious."

"Actually," Kiya said. "Dr. Ace Sr. was the one who asked me to come. He called and invited me personally."

Yara frowned. "He is putting you in Ace's way, I should be mad at Ace Sr.. But on the bright side Ace Jr. has abandoned you, which is quite tacky of him. You are in a crowd of people who you don't know, and he just left you to suffer."

Yara tut-tutted. "Maybe he is not into you. Have you thought of that?"

Kiya shook her head. "I don't think it was like that one of his aunts came and…"

"Don't make up excuses for him." Yara snorted. "I would chalk it up as a man with a poor character trait."

Kiya frowned. "I won't."

"Well, I tried to show you a flaw," Yara sighed. "Come on, I might not like the fact that you are after the man that I am after, and we are in competition, but we'll lay it to the side tonight, and we can hang. I can get to know you better, and you can get to know me better. It's always best to know what the competition is up to,"

Kiya grinned. "So, this was your way of turning me off Ace?"

"Yes," Yara looked at her eagerly, "did it work?"

"No," Kiya shook her head.

"Come along, some church folks are over there. You know them. They're in the choir," Yara said. "I don't want you to be standing around feeling unwelcomed and uncomfortable."

Kiya followed Yara, who carried her to a group of young people from church. It wasn't long before they were engaging her in conversation, and she was feeling quite relaxed.

Yara stayed with the group for a while and then went away to mingle, and Kiya thought that
she actually liked Yara. She was making her intentions about Ace clear, but for some strange reason, she was drawn to her. She might make a good friend.

"Hey, you found friends," Ace said behind her, his breath brushed her ear, and Kiya tingled from her ear down to her toes.

She spun around like she was slapped and stared at Ace transfixed.

"I'll be going to the patio area to practice, are you good here?"

Kiya nodded mutely.

Ace smiled, one of his slow sizzling smiles, and touched her cheek. "I'll be back soon."

Kiya barely breathed out a yes. Her body was on hyperaware mode, just from a tuft of air near her ears.

"So tell me about you, Kiya Brady," Yara said after rejoining the group. A roving waiter served champagne. Kiya declined. She was feeling more hungry than thirsty.

"Why are you in Kingston? I always hear people in the country waxing poetic about how much better it is there."

Kiya laughed. "I think it is better, but I am really a homebody, and that's where I grew up, so I may be biased."

"But you are here," Yara said.

"I needed a break, and I got an excellent job here." Kiya wondered how much of her story she should be telling, Yara did say they were competitors for Ace.

"So why are you still single?" Yara asked. "I heard that the country is overflowing with single men who can't wait to get married."

"I have never heard that. I guess it depends on which area." Kiya laughed. "Well, up until six months ago, I was engaged to be married."

"Ah," Yara looked at her. "Interesting. So, where is he?"

"He married my sister instead." Kiya made a face.

"I feel it for you," Yara said and patted her arm sympathetically. "But listen, Ace has been on my radar for a long, long time before you got here. I have been spending my money going to his practice, making up all sorts of ailments. I can't quit now."

"But does he like you?" Kiya asked.

"Who cares," Yara said. "He'll grow to like me."

"And if he doesn't?"

"Then, there's always DJ." Yara sighed. "Though he has not been on my radar because he has always had his girlfriend, Kelsey. However, she left Jamaica three years ago and married one of DJ's friends. He is still broken-hearted. I don't want to be a rebound girl, and I can almost assure you if Kelsey comes back today, DJ would pick up with her where they left off. I don't want to be involved in that mucky mess."

"Maybe you should look wider," Kiya suggested. "Maybe the Jackson brothers should not be on your radar."

"And maybe you shouldn't be giving me advice since you are a competitor," Yara said good-naturedly. "I threatened to go on a date with Ace, you know, and he finally said yes, so look out Kiya. I am in it to win.

The ushers began seating people, and Kiya went to sit beside Ace, who was at a table at the front. She felt self-conscious doing so, but an usher was told to direct her to sit beside him. It was obviously the family table. She was seated between Ace and Janet, who greeted her quite cordially.

"You look lovely, my dear," Janet said.

"Thank you." Kiya nodded. The MC moved to the front of the stage area and started speaking.

"Four decades ago, boy met girl at the Boston Jerk Festival in Portland. When the boy saw the girl performing with her parents in the popular band Sunny Ray and the Hurricanes, the boy said he stood transfixed he stood still while others were dancing, focused on one particular girl.

Then the boy said, I have to meet that girl.

And when he met her, he realized she was the sister of a love interest of his, Janet.

He was at his wit's end because Janet had all but declared to him that she was going to marry him.

The crowd chuckled.

"The boy went to Janet and said, 'Janet, I am in love with your sister,' Janet stepped aside, gave them her blessings, and six weeks later, Ace Jackson was married to one, Celia Walker. And there began four decades of love and laughter.

"There was never a problem, too huge for this couple, to overcome. Four years after they got married, they had Ace Jr., two years later, Deuce and three years after that, Trey.

Ace Sr. said he was going for five or six, but Celia said no. She wanted to stop at three."

The crowd chuckled again.

Janet leaned toward Kiya and whispered fiercely. "Look at Ace and look at DJ. Do they look anything like Ace Sr.? It's as if they have a totally different father than Trey, doesn't it?"

"Why do you keep saying that?" Kiya whispered, "and what does it have to do with me? Do you think my dad is their father? Is that what this is all about?"

Janet laughed as if she was joining the crowd. "That is exactly what I am implying."

Chapter Eleven

The anniversary party ended way into the night. Kiya was almost comatose by the time Ace dropped her home. She looked at him blearily when he stopped at the gate.

"Why do you still look so preppy and bright? Don't you know the saying, early to bed early to rise, makes a man healthy, wealthy and wise?" Ace smiled, and Kiya could see his white teeth flashing in the half-dark.

"And then there is the saying heights by great men reached and kept were not attained by sudden flight, but they while their companions slept, they were toiling through the night. Who are you going to believe Kiya?

"I am a nocturnal being. I come alive when it's dark."

"Well, I'm the opposite, but thank you for taking me to a nice party. It was really interesting. Your parents have had a full life together, and it was nice to experience a piece of it."

"It was lovely." Ace nodded. "As usual, the Carrs know how to put on a party. I saw you getting chummy with Yara."

"She says we're competitors for your affection." Kiya laughed. "How does it feel to have girls fighting over you?"

"Yara is like a sister," Ace said and then paused.

"And you don't date your sister." Kiya nodded. "I hope you never feel that way about me."

"No, I don't," Ace's expression changed to one of sadness. "Good night, Kiya. Janet told me I didn't have to pick you up tomorrow. She said Nigel's car is ready for you."

"She never told me that," Kiya said. "Thank you so much for picking me up, dropping me back home. I'm sure it was a sacrifice."

"It was no problem," Ace said. "Do you want company for the first drive around this town? I know it can get scary. It's not the same as Portland."

"I'll get by. Besides," Kiya shook her head, "I prefer to make my mistakes alone."

"Call if you get lost," Ace said.

She exited the car, and he waited until she entered the garage apartment. And then he drove away. He had seemed a bit cool to her after the sister joke. Did he believe the crazy notion that her father was his father?

Ace and Deuce looked nothing like her dad, so what Janet was spouting was rubbish.

She couldn't wait to enter her apartment to give her father a call. Maybe he could put some perspective on this.

She knew he'd be up. There were times when he didn't close the shop until around two o'clock in the morning.

Kavina answered his phone instead. "Daddy is in a tournament," Kavina sounded like her usual cranky self, "and they don't seem as if they're going to end tonight."

"Hi, Kav. How are you?" Kiya said.

"You know how I am?" Kavina said grumpily. "Since you moved to Kingston, you haven't even checked up on your sick sister."

"Are you currently sick?" Kiya asked.

"I am always sick, the sickness is inside me," Kavina grumped. "And to make matters worse, Gwen is making me miserable constantly crying and carrying on. I am sure Dad told you that her husband left her."

"I heard. How is she doing?" Kiya asked.

"As if you care," Kavina chuckled. "You should be dancing around and thanking your lucky stars that she is getting the karma she deserves."

"That sounds like something you would do," Kiya said.

"I don't want to talk about Gwen and her constant crying, moaning, and moping," Kavina said. "Tell me about Kingston and other things you've been getting up to. Have you been to a nightclub?"

"No," Kiya said, "but I've been to church. I joined the choir."

"Boring!" Kavina mused. "If I had the opportunity to be away from Dad and Gary, I would live it up."

"And a nightclub is living it up?" Kiya shook her head, knowing her sister couldn't see her.

"I would go out with friends, meet handsome men, do fun city stuff," Kavina said longingly. "Instead, I have to go to the hospital tomorrow for a checkup. Woe is me."

"Maybe you shouldn't still be up," Kiya suggested. "Sleep it off. You won't feel so woeful tomorrow."

"Why do I have to be the one stuck here with sobbing Gwen? If I had her looks and her health, I wouldn't have gone out with Sylvester in the first place. I'd go to the city. I would just probably model or do something fun."

"Kav." Kiya covered a yawn. "Good night, love. Sleep well."

She hung up before Kavina could go on and on about how

her life was a drudgery. She wouldn't dare tell her sister that she got a new wardrobe or that she went to an anniversary party at a mansion. Kavina would launch into one of her woe is me stories.

She wouldn't even tell Gwen, though she dearly wanted to. She didn't want Gwen badgering her to come and live with her in Kingston.

She really needed to talk to her dad and find out why Janet Forbes was constantly suggesting that Ace and Deuce were his children. It would explain a lot. Why Celia Jackson was hostile, why Janet was warning her off Ace, but Ace and Deuce looked nothing like her dad, so all of this was puzzling.

Her dad was short and stocky. He resembled the boxer, Mike Tyson. Come to think of it, none of them resembled their dad. Lorenzo looked nothing like the rest of them. Lorenzo was tall and fair with a narrow face.

Gwen was petite and curvy with grey eyes, caramel complexion, and silky curly hair. Gwen actually looked like she was mixed with some other race, which was curious because both their parents were black. As for Kavina, she was short, skinny, and was lighter in complexion than the rest of them and had a little tilt to her eyes that gave her a catlike appearance.

And Kiya resembled her mom, according to what people said.

But children didn't have to resemble their parents. It was all the luck of the draw when it came to genetics.

She prepared herself for bed. She had a quick shower and slipped into one of Lucia's purchases, a white negligee. She had never worn anything so luxurious feeling to bed before.

She closed her eyes with a smile on her face. Tonight had been very good. She met most of Ace's family. She met his cousin Mason and his wife, Elsa. His Aunt Celine who was not really an aunt but a cousin and his other aunts Carla, Hattie, Beulah, and Camille. They were all nice people, and they were all named from hurricanes.

She closed her eyes and drifted away. She had to wake up early today. It was Marlene's last day, and then she would be the honest to goodness manager of Guy Wiley's farm store.

Kiya Brady, manager of Wiley's Farm Store, the Kingston branch. She turned to her, side punched her pillow, and the next thing she knew, her alarm was going off.

"Five more minutes, you wretched thing," she mumbled. "Thank God, it's Friday."

She barely got through the dressing process.

They practiced casual Fridays, so she pulled on jeans and a polo shirt with the business logo and comfortable wedges.

She almost texted Ace to say she was ready when she remembered that Janet said she could pick up the keys for Nigel's car.

Ace Sr.'s car was in Janet's driveway when she reached the entrance of the house. The front door was left ajar, and Kiya could hear them talking.

"Why are you always upsetting Celia with your innuendoes and insinuations," Ace Sr. was saying.

Janet laughed girlishly. "If she's so upset, why isn't she the one here trying to make me see the errors of my ways."

"Did she tell you what I was supposed to have done to upset her highness?" Janet asked.

"No," Ace Sr. said, "she just said you were rude as usual and a know-it-all who shouldn't have retired because you have nothing better to do than to upset her. I tend to agree."

"All I did was ask her if I could tell Kiya the truth," Janet said innocently.

"The truth about what?" Ace Sr. asked. Kiya was about to

call out to let them know she was there, but she pushed the door and tiptoed a little bit closer.

"The truth about everything," Janet said lightly. "The truth you do not want to address because you have your head squarely in the sand, but there are consequences, Norman. People with their heads in the sand can cause stuff like incest. Of course, Celia wouldn't say anything," Janet said grumpily. "She will keep her secrets until the day she dies. That stupid woman is going to mess up Ace's life."

"Don't call my wife stupid."

Kiya peered around the corner and saw that Ace Sr. was bandaging Janet's foot.

"I can call her anything I want," Janet said, "I've been calling her stupid from the day she started acting stupidly. If you had married me, you wouldn't be second-guessing about your sons."

"I am not second-guessing about my son's," Ace said through gritted teeth.

"I think," Janet said, "that you want to see how this ends up too. You know the wife you have, and you are pushing Kiya into Aces' arms because you want your wife to stop it."

"Your foot looks none the worse for wear." Ace Sr. stood up. "I really don't know why you didn't call the other Ace. I told him I wanted to have nothing to do with you."

"But what about the Hippocratic Oath?" Janet said, innocently. "Didn't you swear to do no harm, to help those that were in need?"

Ace Sr. sighed. "If I never have to see you or your foot again, it would be too soon."

"Bah," Janet said, fanning him off. "You are just angry because you don't know what your wife has been up to in the past. Tell the truth, Norman. It has been eating you up inside. Maybe Kiya is your salvation. The final revelation."

Kiya cleared her throat. Janet looked across at her. "Oh, there you are. Nigel's key is right on that keyring behind you. And the papers are on the counter, insurance, license, that kind of thing. Is your driver's license up to date?"

"Yes, ma'am." Kiya nodded. "Good morning to you both."

"Good morning, Kiya," Ace Sr. said. "You see, I had to make this morning call because Ace was unavailable. He had an emergency early this morning with a patient, so I was stuck with this one. This conspiracy theorist." He shook his head. "Discount everything you have heard her say about anything. She's a lovely person because she has the Walker blood in her, so she'll be kind, but I think Janet is going a little senile."

"No, I'm not," Janet said. "You would love to think so, but I am quite sane. There is nothing wrong with me, but these toes, I seem to have kinda disturbed them last night."

"Only a senile person would dance on toes that they're not supposed to. You keep doing the same thing to them." Ace Sr. grunted.

"I called my father last night to ask him if he was the father of Ace and Deuce," Kiya blurted out.

Ace Sr. stopped in his tracks and look back at her. "You see what you've done, you madwoman. Look at the child, calling her father, asking him foolish questions."

Janet frowned. "I didn't mean for her to do that."

"Well, I'm confused," Kiya said. "I'm just confused."

"That's Janet for you, confusing." Ace Sr. rolled his eyes and headed for the bathroom.

Kiya took the keys. "Thank you, Janet. This means so much to me."

"I know child, no thanks necessary," Janet said. "We've all been there. We've all come from the country to the town and had to struggle a bit. Well, not Celine. You met

Celine last night. She and Celia are as tight as two cows in a cowshed. When she came to Kingston, that's Celine, she had a wealthy benefactor who gave her an apartment, cars, clothes, education, while the rest of us had to struggle."

Kiya stood by politely, wondering when it would be best to leave. Obviously, Janet had more problems with her sisters than Kiya had with hers.

"Do you know who Celine's wealthy benefactor was?" Janet asked. "You remember that charming gentleman that came to our table and said some sweet sugary crap?"

Kiya nodded. "That's senator, Toddy Pryce."

Janet nodded. "That's the one. He was Celine's lover for years before she finally married him."

"Oh really..." Kiya stuttered.

"Celine and Celia are cut off the same cloth?" Janet said peevishly,

"Celine is your niece?" Kiya said, trying to put it all together. Their family was large.

"Yes! Celine was my brother Charles' girl. Charles died when he was seventeen. Our parents grew Celine like she was their own. Technically she's a niece and not a sister. The both of them Celine and Celia were young and full of power over men," Janet said bitterly.

"Okay, that's enough." Ace Sr. came into the hallway. "Let the girl go to work, Janet, and stop splashing your jealousy all over her. Do you see that, Kiya?" Ace Sr. pointed at Janet. "Do you see that around her mouth. It's turning green— green with envy. Green with jealousy. Green with her stupid theories." He headed through the door, and Janet threw a magazine at him.

Kiya shook her head. "Goodbye, Janet. Have a nice day."

"Oh, I will," Janet yelled. "I know who my children's father is."

The garage opener was on the key ring. Kiya opened the garage and headed to Nigel's car.

"Do you want to follow me in traffic?" Ace Sr. asked jovially. Obviously, the confrontation with Janet was not affecting him at all, "I'll lead you through."

"Thank you." Kiya nodded. "I was feeling a little bit nervous."

"I know. I can tell." He winked at her and went into the vehicle. Kiya backed out of the garage, narrowly missing one of Janet's hibiscus plant. She followed Ace Sr. onto the road, and he slowly winded his way through traffic. He stopped in front of her workplace and gave her a thumbs up.

"You have a good day, Kiya. And don't for a minute internalize any of the nonsense Janet is spewing, okay?"

Kiya nodded. "Okay."

Chapter Twelve

Ace knocked on DJ's apartment door. It was time for their weekly tennis match. DJ opened the door and was already in his truck suit.

"You are early this evening," Deuce grinned.

"No, I'm not early, I'm actually late," Ace said. "You have your clock still set on daylight saving time? Is your watch not working?"

Deuce looked back on his clock and said, "Yes, for real, it's not working, and I did take a little nap."

"Come on," Ace said. "Enough of the talking. Let's go beat some ball."

Instead of the elevator, they took the stairwell. It was their way to warm up.

"It was a nice anniversary party, wasn't it?" Deuce said. "I haven't gotten a chance to talk to you since.

"It was good," Ace shrugged. "Mom looked a little apprehensive in some parts of it, didn't you think?"

"No," DJ stopped on a step and stretched. "What are you getting on about?"

"To me, she looked a little guilty, especially when they were talking about Portland and back in the day."

"You are imagining things," Deuce chuckled. "Mom did not look guilty or apprehensive. She was happy and bubbly, the same as she always is."

"Okay, if you say so."

They began the game, but Ace realized that Deuce was distracted. He beat him in two straight sets.

"Now I may be wrong about Mom and the anniversary party, but you are distracted," Ace said.

"Kelsey is back," Deuce panted.

"Back in Jamaica?" Ace asked.

"Yup," Deuce said. "And divorced."

"I guess this means you are going back to her?" Ace joked. "What are you going to do? You have two ladies now, that girl you've been obsessing over that you have never met, and Kelsey, the woman who can do anything, and you still take her back."

DJ pause as if he was contemplating what he said.

"It was a joke," Ace said appalled. "You should laugh and reassure me that you don't know the text pal, but you do know Kelsey. You two were joined at the hip, and you two always seem to end up back together..."

"I don't know about getting back with Kelsey," Deuce said, "she got married to someone else. That was a big deal. Before she broke up with me, she essentially said I was boring, and she wanted to meet new people and be in other relationships."

"You told me you told her it was fine; she was to do what she wanted." Ace said.

"But I never expected her to actually do it." Deuce shook

his head. "And now she's back and single. She texted me, do you know what she said?"

"Maybe we can pick up where we left off DJ, I am sorry, and she signed it love Kelsey."

"You have never had a problem with that in the past." Ace said, "you two were always breaking up and getting back together. It's what you are known for your roller-coaster relationship."

"I am tired of it, I hopped off the roller coaster when she got married to my friend to spite me."

"Your ego is hurt," Ace said.

"My ego was hurt three years ago," Deuce muttered. "My ego is not hurt now."

"You still love her."

"I'm not sure about that." Deuce frowned.

"Where is she practicing?" Ace asked.

"Sunrise Medical." Deuce snorted. "They welcomed her back with open arms."

"Everybody needs some time away. I heard her say from each other," Ace started singing.

"Oh, stop it," Deuce growled. "The hook of that song says, and after all that's been said and done, you're just a part of me I can't let go... I'm not sure if I share those sentiments anymore. Maybe I am cured of the Kelsey spell."

"It's that Phantom girl you've been talking to that's making you feel that way. She has replaced Kelsey in your affections."

"Maybe," Deuce said. "I think she's more my type. I know I haven't met her in person, but I can just feel it."

Ace slung a towel around his neck and rubbed it rhythmically. "Modern relationships are hard for me to wrap my head around. He has never met the girl, and yet he feels as if they're compatible."

Deuce grinned. "So, how is your traditional relationship going with Kiya?"

"We're not in a relationship." Ace frowned. "She's just a friend. I like her. I like hanging out with her, and for the past week, I've been taking her around the city. I promise to take her to Golden Acres tomorrow. By the way, you haven't visited in a while."

"I have two more months of hospital duty before David gets back, then I'll take some time for myself, and I'll be visiting Golden Acres. You should make a move on Kiya, though. It's obvious you like her."

"I can't make a move on Kiya." Ace shrugged. "I have doubts."

"Doubts about what?" Deuce asked. "Does she take drugs? Is she a prostitute or a stripper on the side?"

Ace sighed. "Don't you find it weird how we resemble the Wileys and not our own father. And don't you find it bizarre that Dad stopped going to Portland, a place he still waxes poetic about every chance he gets?"

Deuce folded his arms and then raised his eyebrows. "All of Dad's family died. There is nobody there for him to visit. There is no one to go back to. And as far as us resembling the Wileys, I don't understand."

"Trey is his favorite son because Trey resembles Dad." Ace said.

"Trey needed more attention. He was wild when he was younger. You and I were different," Deuce countered. "We didn't need the kind of attention Trey got. But now Trey is back in line, and Dad is not paying him as much attention. Do you realize that?"

"Well, you have a point, sounds like you bought that line from dad," Ace said. "However, how do you explain away the fact that Mom doesn't want to say if she ever cheated or not?"

"Now that is strange," Deuce said. "I've never heard that before. Mom cheated on Dad, with who?"

"I asked her if she has ever cheated, and she doesn't want to say. Read into that what you will," Ace said. "If somebody didn't cheat on their spouse, they would readily say that they didn't, not Mom. She deflects, she beats around the bush, and she looks like somebody who has been caught with her hand in the cookie jar. That, coupled with the fact that Micky Wiley was our gardener before we were born."

"Not that nonsense again," Deuce said. "Aunt Janet has been harping on about that for years—her little conspiracy theory. Dad said to ignore it, and I've been doing that. I can't believe you have taken that up now."

"DJ, I know you have analytical skills," Ace said heavily. "Analyze this, Micky Wiley was the gardener, and Dad was working at the hospital at the time and was hardly home. Mom was at home. We look like the gardener, DJ. You and I have his eyes."

Deuce sighed. "What does all of this have to do with Kiya? The original question I asked was, why weren't you making a move on Kiya?"

"Because Kiya's mother had a relationship with Micky Wiley too."

"Oh." Deuce nodded. "I see where this is coming from. So you think Micky Wiley is our biological father, and you think Kiya is Micky Wiley's biological daughter. Ergo, we are brother and sister."

"Ha, he has seen the light," Ace said sarcastically.

"I don't believe any of this nonsense," Deuce said. "I have no time for these kinds of things. Ace, where do you get the time? I know you have a busy practice."

"So you think I should just forget all about this?" Ace

asked. "What if you found out that Kelsey was your sister?" Kelsey, whom you've been with for over ten years?"

"It would be disturbing, especially because Kelsey and I have had sex," Deuce said, "but it's not possible."

"It was just an example." Ace sat on the bench at the side of the tennis court. "I can't really wrap my mind around all of this either, you know. This kind of thing gives me no joy, no joy at all. Mom won't admit to any of this. Dad is in flat out denial. You know, I was the one who had to go back to Portland, close down the practice, and put that house up for sale. He didn't even want to set a foot back in Portland. The other day he made a joke that Mom had her eyes on Micky Wiley, and Mom got all jittery and uncomfortable."

"There is something there, DJ; we can't afford to ignore this."

Deuce sat beside him. "So we should test everybody. You test Kiya, me, you, and Micky Wiley. Put all of this nonsense to rest. It has been dragging on too long. We're in our thirties, and if you're so troubled about it, then you need answers."

"Mom said I shouldn't go there, and I promised her."

"What Mom is doing is extracting a promise from you to not do anything about it, but it is not right," Deuce said. "because she wants to pretend that nothing happened. Do you realize if we're not our father's children that their marriage is a sham? All of the anniversary lovey-dovey stuff was just a lie."

"I think they love each other, "Ace said. They worked it out after many years. Why else would they still be together?"

After the tennis match with Deuce, Ace texted Kiya on a whim?

"Are you hungry? It's grill night at the Waterfall."

Kiya texted back: *yes, I am hungry, and grill night sounds amazing.*

It didn't take him long to reach Janet's house from DJ's. Kiya was waiting for him at the gate in jeans and a red top that hugged her curves lovingly.

"Red looks good on you." He smiled. "But then again, everything looks good on you."

"Thank you," Kiya said. "Everything looks good on you too."

"We are a mutual admiration society." Ace chuckled.

"I had to feed your aunt Janet's cat. She went out with her daughter, Sandy, and won't be back until the end of the week."

"So you will be home alone," Ace said.

"I've never been home alone." Kiya made a face. "I am always reassured that you're Aunt Janet is just next door."

"You'll get used to it. There's nothing to fear."

"If you say so."

"Nothing ever happens in this neighborhood," Ace said.

"Until it happens to me," Kiya said and immediately regretted her negativity. "Don't mind me. Apparently, some of Kavina's negativity is rubbing off on me."

"That's the sister who is perpetually unhappy?" Ace asked.

"That's her. I know other people who have sickle cell, and they are nothing like grumpy Kavina. Nothing makes that girl happy. And I don't want to be like that. I don't want to be sitting here and complaining when I know I am blessed."

"Yes, you are, and you'll do fine," Ace said, "But on the off chance that you're not, I'll come stay with you, carry some board games, and what not. We can play or watch TV until you decide that you want to sleep."

"Thank you, Ace. I mean it. Thank you so much. "

****

It was a Reggae themed grill night at the Waterfalls. The

decorations were red, yellow, and green, and the mellow reggae music greeted them as they entered.

"I want to sing karaoke," Kiya said, her face lighting up.

"You are more excited about the singing than the food, aren't you?" Ace grinned.

"You'll be pleased to know they have prizes."

"Prizes!" Kiya's face lit up. "Like what?"

"Like a dinner for two here or a free dessert. I've never managed to win one of these prizes. Somebody with a better voice has always beaten me out. One night I went up against Case Wiley and another night Peter Wiley, they have no business doing karaoke here."

"Maybe we should sing together," Kiya said. "And double our chances for success."

"Unfortunately, my favorite song is not a duet." Ace shook his head.

"What is your favorite song?" Kiya asked curiously. She was expecting something along the lines of R and B.

Ace grinned, "I know what you are thinking, and you are wrong. My favorite song, believe it or not, is Junior Gong's Affairs of Heart. I just think it's a beautiful love song,"

"It is one of mine too." Kiya nodded," my dad used to play it all the time at the shop, and I know the lyrics by heart. I used to imagine a guy singing it to me and telling me that my love is life-changing, and he wouldn't be the same without me, darling." Kiya laughed self-consciously. "I am a closet romantic."

"There's nothing wrong with that," Ace looked at her contemplatively. "Do you realize that there's a line in that song that says, 'the last person you are with, made a big mistake, he missed out something that's great'?

Kiya nodded and then laughed. "Oh yes, my favorite part in my present circumstances."

"I'll sing it for you," Ace winked at her. "When I sing that line, you know I am talking about you."

Kiya blushed. "Well… er…"

"What are you singing?" Ace asked to put her back at ease.

"Dreamland by Marcia Griffiths." Kiya grimaced, "I am afraid, you can't win with me singing that song. It is my all-time favorite. I don't even need a karaoke machine to give me the words."

"Okay, let the games begin." They thumped their fists together. "Let's see who wins."

"Can we sing first?" Kiya asked. "I don't do too well on a full stomach.

"Okay, we'll sign up for the competition." They headed to the table where the person was taking names for the competition.

They would have to wait until the person who was currently singing was finished. Still, Ace reasoned that that person was no competition at all.

She was singing Someone Loves You Honey by JC Lodge. Even the soothing sounds of the reggae music could not drown out the disservice that the singer was doing to the song.

He and Kiya looked at each other and started laughing.

"How many people are in the segment of the competition?" Kiya asked the girl who greeted them. Her name tag said, Rose.

"Just six," Rose said. "First prize is a dinner for two tonight. The second prize is a lunch special, and when I say free dinner," Rose said, "I mean drinks, dessert and everything that's included, all taxes and charges paid."

Kiya nodded eagerly. "That sounds great, and you say just six competitors for this segment?"

"Well, including you two, it would be eight," Rose said.

"Are you signing up?"

"Oh, yes." Kiya nodded eagerly. "Oh, yes sign me up. I am Kiya Brady."

"Ace Jackson," Ace said.

"Kiya, what would you like to sing," Rose said. "So, we can put the music up for you."

"Dreamland, Marcia Griffiths," Kiya said.

"And Ace?" Rose looked at him.

"Affairs of the Heart by Junior Gong Marley."

"Good luck," Rose smiled. "Kiya is up next and then you Ace. The patron's vote after every delivery. The person with the most votes at the end of this segment wins."

Kiya sang her song, and she sounded very good, as he knew she would. She got a rousing applause when she was finished. She made a little bow and then walked off this stage.

"Beat that, Ace Jackson!"

Ace laughed. "Pride cometh before a fall."

"In that case, I repent." Kiya gave him a mock contrite look, "something tells me you are about to kill it out there."

"I should," Ace winked at her, "I am dedicating it to you."

She stood on the outskirts of the karaoke area when Ace started the song.

By the time he was at the second verse, people were standing up and clapping and singing along. Ace had to admit that the guitar solo helped him along. People were rocking and into the music.

When he finished, there were shouts for an encore. Rose met him before he came off the stage and shook his hand.

"That was awesome! A free dinner for you and your partner!"

"Shouldn't you be waiting on the votes?" Ace chuckled, "I thought there was a system."

"Redundant, I am sure." Rose winked at him. "You have a

nice voice, and you deejay well. You could give Junior Gong a run for his money."

"Thank you." Ace saw Kiya heading toward him a smile on her face.

"That was great," Kiya hugged him. A full-body hug that had all her curves fitting perfectly into him.

It was a brief and spontaneous, but so impactful he felt staggered for a while. He almost didn't hear what she said next.

"It's not fair," Kiya said good-naturedly. "You killed it like you've practiced this before."

"I've done it before at a wedding or two at a groom's request." Ace said huskily, "It's not a traditional love song, but I think the words are quite sentimental."

"And you dedicated it to me," Kiya whispered. "I like that."

Ace stared at her transfixed for a while, he could see himself applying some of those words to her. Lord, help him.

"Sharon will see you to your table." Rose interrupted their frozen tableau.

Something significant had passed between them. He knew she felt it too.

Chapter Thirteen

It was a week of fun and games, literally. Kiya and Ace watched movies together, played games together. He knew so many card games, it was unbelievable.

"My family is big on card games if you can't tell by our names," Ace grinned.

He taught her how to play poker, and they had a running poker tournament with just the two of them. They chatted late into the night, and sometimes they listened to music and then had impromptu karaoke.

It was literally the best week of Kiya's life.

On the last night before Janet returned, and Ace was no longer obligated to keep her company, they went to Devon House to get ice cream. They both had the same preferred flavor, cookies and cream. They walked and chatted in the balmy night.

For Kiya, this was bliss. She never once thought about Sylvester and Gwen or any of that nonsense that took her to

Kingston. It seemed like it was way in the past, even though it was just a few weeks.

"Remember that Marcia Griffith's song that I sang at karaoke night at the Waterfalls?" Kiya asked.

"I remember," Ace said. "You did a great job with it. I love that song."

"I think I'm living it," Kiya said. "This is my dreamland. I don't want it to be over."

Ace looked at her pensively. "I understand how you feel. I enjoyed hanging with you this week too, I like your company more than I like anyone else's in my life."

"It's crazy. I was engaged to Sylvester for five years, and now I don't even think about him."

Ace inhaled raggedly. "Kiya, we should talk."

It was a conversation he was skirting around for weeks. Even while they were together and she laughed over something, or he watched her as she thought of something, he searched for familiar features to himself.

He was caught in a loop of denial and desire.

He wanted to believe his mother that he was a Jackson, and yet at the back of his mind, there was a niggling doubt that was not going away.

He had allowed this to happen. They were spending an inordinate amount of time together. They had a lot of things in common. The familiarity was breathing an attachment that he should not have started. It was all his fault.

He didn't have to spend time with Kiya, while Janet was away. Nothing would have happened to her, the place was perfectly safe, but like a homing pigeon, he found himself going to her place after work, cooking with her and playing games. Basically, living in domestic bliss, nurturing feelings that had now blossomed into something else other than mere attraction. And now they were locked in their dreamland together.

It was only a dream. Well, it was only a dream until he got to the bottom of this, and he would. He had made up his mind that he would really get to the bottom.

Kiya elbowed him while he wrangled in his head what he was going to say to her about their situation. This was not only about him and his paternity. This was also about her, and she adored her father.

"Yes, I was thinking…" Ace began. His phone rang, saving him from saying something stupid, but it wasn't anyone to rescue him from having a conversation he didn't want to have, it was Yara.

"I finally figured out where I want us to go for a date," Yara said before he could even say hello.

"Where?" Ace asked cautiously.

"I think we should be casual and laid back, no pressure. What about Devon House? We could go for ice cream and walk around in the park this Saturday night."

Ace almost choked.

"Sure." If only Yara could see his expression now. He was at Devon House with Kiya.

"And if we find that we really do not have anything going on between us," Yara said, "then we cool it. I will back away and give Kiya free reign to you."

Ace wanted to ask her why she believed Kiya wanted free reign to him, but he resisted. Kiya was walking beside him.

"Okay. Saturday night is a date," he said and hung up.

Kiya looked across at him. "That's Yara, isn't it?"

"Same one," Ace said. "She said we needed to date and find out if we have anything going between us."

A sharp pang of jealousy hit Kiya out of nowhere. She knew it was coming, Yara had told her, but somehow, she didn't expect it to hurt this much.

"Do you like her?" Kiya asked the jealousy seeped into her voice.

"I like her as a person. She's a beautiful woman and funny and smart, but as I said before, she's like a little sister to me. My mother and her mom have been friends for years."

"I sit beside her brother's fiancée in the choir," Kiya said. "She says their family is loving and caring and all kinds of awesome."

"They are lovely family," Ace said, "but Yara has had a crush on me for years, and I know it, and she knows that I know it. I guess you can't manufacture chemistry and attraction, can you? No matter how attractive they are, you are drawn to some people, and you just not drawn to others, at least not in the way that they would want you to let them. It's just a fact of life."

Kiya nodded. "I get it. I know what you are talking about. It doesn't make me feel any less jealous about you and Yara still."

Ace reached for her hand and squeeze her fingers. It was the first time he was initiating physical contact with her. It started a trembling in his body, a physical reaction that surprised him.

He thought that he had gotten over this adolescent feeling. He wasn't in puberty. He was a man nearing his forties, and yet, the touch of a woman's hand couldn't make him feel trembly inside.

He let her fingers go. It was becoming too unbearable. Now he knew why the older generation had chaperones and didn't want to allow their young people alone with each other. He had never felt this physical reaction before.

"So, are we still on for Golden Acres tomorrow night?" Ace asked, trying to change the subject.

"Sure," Kiya said. "I am looking forward to meeting your

Aunt Florence. That story you told me about her finding her sister after fifty-odd years is amazing. And her sister losing her memory permanently. You never hear these things outside of books or movies."

"It happens," Ace said. "Aunt Florence has a new lease on life, I tell you. She's literally floating. She went on a cruise with Heather Grayson the other day. Just the two of them on Heather Grayson's yacht. She said she brought back souvenirs from the French Riviera."

"A yacht? Her sister is rich?" Kiya opened her eyes.

"Yes. Her sister's husband's nickname is Midas."

"What a find. And she's also Guy Wiley's grandmother? My boss's grandmother has a yacht."

"Guy is rich in his own right," Ace said. "I doubt if he's excited about his grandmother having a yacht."

"You know there was a time when I didn't think he was rich? Guy surely doesn't act like it. Lucia is coming by to pick me up on Saturday, and I'll be spending Saturday and Sunday with her and Guy. She'll be dropping the children off to be with their Wiley relatives."

"I knew Lucia would end up taking care of Novalee's daughter," Ace said. "I was around a couple years ago when that drama went down. I actually thought I had a chance with Lucia then,"

"You loved her?"

"At the time, I did. She's a beautiful person inside and out. You know that.? There's something about the girls from the Rio Grande Valley area."

Kiya fanned her face. "Were amazing, aren't we? But then again, your mother and aunts are from that area, so you're just complimenting your own family."

"There is that." Ace chuckled. "Anyway, enjoy your stay with Lucia and Guy. I know you will. I will miss you. I've been hanging out with you every day this week. I'm going to feel lonely."

"You will have Yara for company Saturday night."

"It is not what you think it's going to be," Ace said. "Yara and I will go out, and she'll realize that I'm pretty boring, and she can do better."

Kiya snorted. "Yeah right? You might just find out that you like Yara after all."

"Not going to happen with you around," Ace looked at her longingly. "I highly doubt it."

****

Golden Acres was a resort unlike anything that Kiya had ever expected for this kind of business. Ace had picked her up from work. He said his aunt Florence was expecting them for dinner.

"This is yours?" She whispered, looking around at the rustic yet elegant exterior.

"I co-own it with Quade," Ace said. "You met Quade at the anniversary party?"

"Yes, I did. The guy that looked like LL Cool J with hazel eyes?"

"You think Quade looks like LL Cool J?" Ace laughed and hit the steering wheel.

"Why is his name Quade? Doesn't Quade mean fourth," Kiya mused. "You are Ace, your brother is Deuce, your other brother is Trey I get that, but why is he Quade? He is not a brother."

"Because my mother named him," Ace laughed. "She was good friends with her sister-in-law, and Aunt Cherry was quite happy to go along with it. If she hadn't died, there would probably have been a Quincy, and the list would go on and on. They were pretty dedicated to it."

Florence Jackson's cottage was a neat place that had lavender plants at the front.

"She's a lavender fan," Ace said. Florence already had a visitor who opened the door and greeted them jovially.

"Hi Ace, and this must be Kiya."

"Hey Danica," Ace said. "Yes, this is Kiya. Kiya, this is Danica."

Danica was fascinating to look at, her skin was golden brown and seemed as if it were glowing, her hair was varying shades of brown and her eyes a lighter brown than her hair.

"I have heard about you before Danica," Kiya said, "you are Guy Wiley's cousin, he is my boss. She isn't your cousin too, is she?" Kiya asked Ace confused.

"Not that I know of," Ace said, "but anything can happen in my family tree."

Danica chuckled. "Come on in, guys. Maybe Ace can explain the complex family tree to you."

It was a spacious cottage with an open plan area. From the front door to the back door was a large patio that open to some mountain views. It was chilly, something that Kiya didn't expect in April.

"It's always chilly up here," Danica said as if reading her mind. "Didn't you tell her to take a sweater, Ace?"

"I don't feel it anymore, so it completely slipped my mind, sorry, Kiya."

"It's not too bad," Kiya said.

"I am going to lend you one of Aunt Florence's shawls." Danica disappeared into one of the bedrooms and came back out with a pretty grey shawl.

Kiya put it on and instantly felt better.

Florence Jackson was in the kitchen; she came out wiping her hands on a tablecloth.

"Ace, my baby! I have so many stories to tell you."

"I can imagine," Ace said, going over to hug and kiss her on the cheeks.

"We sailed around on this giant yacht. Oh my goodness, Ace. I didn't know luxury like this existed in this world. Where are my manners? Hello Kiya. It's lovely of you to come over."

"Hello," Kiya said. "Ace told me about you, and I wanted to meet you."

"Oh, I love her, Ace," Florence said, hugging Kiya. "In case you're wondering, I did not cook. I sent it to the restaurant for food. It's luxurious takeaway that I was arranging on platters." Florence winked at Kiya.

"Let's go eat on the veranda. Tell me some more about Portland and I'll tell you about the French Riviera."

The food was good, really good. It was on the level of the Waterfalls food that they had the a few nights before.

Kiya was impressed. "Can an ordinary customer visit the Golden Acres restaurant?" Kiya asked, after she cut a slice of succulent baked chicken.

"No," Danica was the one who responded. "But let me tell you something. I'm quite happy that I have an active job because I've been eating my soul away up here."

"So, what exactly do you do?" Kiya asked.

"I am the entertainment coordinator for the residents. And I do entertain my poor clients. I keep them on their toes." Danica chuckled. "I hear them calling me the energy bunny. We do different tours around Jamaica. You can come on one or two are all of them if you desire, it's fun."

"And she's not just saying that because Ace is at the table," Florence said. "She genuinely likes these people."

"I would consider doing the tours," Kiya said, "but I don't know when I'd have the time to do it, probably on a holiday or something. The farm store is surprisingly active."

"How is that going?" Danica asked,

"I love it," Kiya said, "I love being around the plants. I especially love to see the plants in rehabilitation come back to life. We get them busted up and mangled looking, I enjoy seeing them become robust and strong again. We also have regular plants, but I especially enjoy seeing the ones that don't look too good make a comeback."

"I understand how you feel completely," Florence said. "Working with nature is like the best job that you can have. You should be friends with Celia and Celine. They love people who garden," Florence said.

"I don't think Celia likes me," Kiya said.

"Why ever not?" Florence protested. "Celia likes everybody."

"And that's a conversation for another time." Ace sighed. "Tell us more about Heather Grayson's yacht."

Florence was only willing to change this subject.

"It's huge," she said. "And they have staff on there that are there to serve anything you fancy."

"I can't wait for the family trip," Danica said. "My mom and Aunt Sharla are positively chomping at the bit for it."

"Sounds fun," Kiya said wistfully. "It would be nice to do something like that with my family."

"For a long time, we didn't know each other," Danica said. "A lot of us didn't know we were related."

"Don't sound so envious. At least you grew up with your family," Ace cleared his throat.

Florence looked at him sharply.

Kiya didn't miss that look, and she wondered. Was Ace still hung up on what Janet said about him and his brother Deuce having another father?

While they were in the car going home, she asked him.

"You know you get agitated every time my family comes up. It's beginning to get suspicious, Ace. Do you think my father is your father too?"

"Your father, as in George Brady?" Ace asked. "No, I don't think so."

"Well then, stop acting suspiciously every time my family comes up," Kiya said. "You and your aunt are going to give me a complex."

"Okay. I'll try to stop acting suspiciously." Ace mused, "but I guess Aunt Janet is in my head a little. You can't blame me for being a little uncomfortable, can you?"

"No," Kiya chuckled, "but wouldn't it be strange if we were brother and sister? It would be really, really strange. I would have to flush my thoughts and emotions. I'd probably have to run back to Portland. Ace Jackson, my brother. It would be the end of the world."

Ace looked at her solemnly and didn't say a word.

Chapter Fourteen

Lucia came to pick up Kiya for the weekend. She had her niece and her son with her in the back.

Her son looked like a curly-haired cherub, a mini Guy Wiley with just a dash of Lucia.

"Meet Joseph Michael and Crystal," Lucia said.

"Joseph looks like a Guy clone," Kiya grinned. "I just want to pinch his little chubby cheeks, and Crystal is your mother's twin with Earl's complexion."

"Sorry that these two won't be around for the weekend, you'll get to know them at another time, but they have two birthday parties to attend at the Wiley Complex with their cousins."

"I've heard about the Wiley Complex," Kiya said. "Ace said it's a place where all the Wiley's live like a tribe."

"Well, not all of us live there, obviously," Lucia said. "Guy and I spend most of our time on the farm. Guy has a townhouse there that he keeps for friends or relatives who are visiting, his cousin Danica is staying there now. If you hadn't gotten a place to stay, that is exactly where you would be too. If I had found out that you had problems at your father's friends."

Kiya smiled at her. "You are so caring and considerate."

"It's some of Guy rubbing off on me." Lucia grinned.

"Auntie Lucia, I'm thirsty." Crystal interrupted.

"We're almost there." Lucia looked back at her niece. "When we get there, you can get one of the juices, I packed for you.

"She has a thing about being thirsty, but what she really wants is the strawberry juice that I made for her," Lucia said under her breath, "I have my niece hooked on strawberry juice."

Kiya grinned. "You are a bad aunt; you have her hooked on sugary drinks."

"No sugar added," Lucia said, "just straight strawberries from the overripe berries. She loves it."

Lucia looked back at Crystal who was listening.

"Aunty Lucia does the best drinks."

She had her father's smile. Kiya thought.

"How are your brothers Earl? And Nate?" Kiya asked, turning around again. "I haven't seen them in a while."

"Earl is still working in St Ann; he got a promotion the other day, so he is busy like a bee," Lucia said. "And Nate is finishing med school."

"I heard your mother is getting married again." Kiya murmured. "And will be moving from Portland. My dad gets all the juicy news."

"Yes, she is getting married in the summer to a school principal. He lives in Montego Bay. We like him," Lucia made a face. "But mom has turned into a bridezilla, one would think this was her first wedding. It is his first marriage, so I am not sure if that is why she is acting so over the top. I'll tell you more after I drop off these Munchkins."

Lucia turned into a gated area with palm trees at the front. The Wiley Complex was like a resort area.

Kiya looked around and shook her head. "Oh boy, this is nice."

"I know. Come on in and meet the designer. She is the babysitter for the weekend."

Kiya met Shawn Wiley, who gave her a quick hug. They exchanged pleasantries, and Lucia said she would be back tomorrow.

"Fine, fine," Shawn said. "They will be in one piece."

Shawn kissed Joseph Michael on his chubby cheeks. "I may not want to give back this chunky cutie pie."

Joseph wrapped his hands around her and snuggled in her neck.

"Traitor," Lucia murmured.

Kiya laughed.

When Lucia was driving out, she sighed. "Shawn is the best, I tell you. I don't worry when I leave my children here."

"You think of Crystal as yours? Kiya raised a brow.

"I am beginning to." Lucia made a face. "Neither Nova nor Earl checks in to find out how she is doing." Lucia sighed. "Nova hasn't seen Crystal in six months, and I'm the one who has to bring up her name in conversations. I don't know what kind of mother Nova is."

"Maybe like mine was," Kiya said sadly. "I don't remember my mom; I see a hazy picture or two, and everybody says I resemble her, but that is all."

"And that's why I think you're going to love this weekend," Lucia said. "Guy and I were thinking of doing a homecoming magazine to highlight the businesses and the people of the Rio Grande valleys. We got a lot of pictures from the old days. Maybe you can find your mom in one or two of them.

"I saw your father. There was a picture of him standing in front of the shop when it was like a small board structure. And he had an afro and was wearing bell-bottoms." Lucia laughed and hit the steering wheel. "Man, those were the days. You know, George's shop was where everything happened."

"Yup," Kiya nodded. "It still is the place where everything happens."

"You know, your father was the reason why we could eat several nights when we just moved to the valleys." Lucia looked at her sideways. "He was so kind to us. There was no Farm Help Society then and the neighborhood rallied around us, especially him. That is why, I do not want to hear a word from you about anything I do for you being too much. Got that, Miss Kiya?"

"Got it." Kiya nodded.

The road leading up to Guy's place was picturesque, there were rows of mango trees, for as far as the eye could see. There was a separate entrance to the greenhouses, she couldn't wait to see inside them. That was where most of the store supplies came from.

She was getting excited. She wound down the window and sniffed the air. The closer they got to the house on the hill, the headier the scent of strawberries became.

"We basically have strawberries year-round," Lucia said. "There is always a variety in season as you know, you sell the suckers and probably know more about it than I do."

"If I lived here, I would be red from strawberry eating," Kiya was sniffing the air like a hound. "I love this place."

"I knew you would," Lucia said smugly. "That is why you need to come visit often. I hope you were taking note of the route to get here, so you can visit on your own."

Guy greeted them at the door. Kiya was struck again by how handsome he was. Guy Wiley was in a league of his own when it came to male beauty, and yet she had never been even remotely attracted to him, not like she was with Ace. He was very good to look at, but that was about it for her.

He hugged Lucia, then he hugged her.

"Marlene said you are a perfect replacement for her," Guy said. "And I am just so relieved that things are working out." He grinned at Kiya. "Because if you hadn't worked out, I don't know what Lucia would do to me if I had to voice my displeasure."

Lucia grinned. "Come on, Kiya. "You have a lot of touring to do. And then we can have some wine on the back patio and chat."

It turned out to be quite the weekend with Lucia and Guy. He teased her about liking Ace, his former love rival.

"Does that mean that Ace Jackson is going to be back in my life?" Guy mused. "Are we going to have to be friends now?"

Lucia pinched him. "It's possible, Kiya likes him, and he likes her, and we are Kiya's friends."

Kiya blushed while they were talking. To be honest, she could imagine the four of them hanging out and having dinner together.

"Does Ace still have that Bob Marley quote hanging in his car?" Lucia asked Kiya.

Kiya nodded. "The one that says, if she is amazing, she won't be easy, and if she's easy, she won't be amazing… If she's worthy, you won't give up, and if you give up, you are not worthy? Yup, he still has it."

"I love that quote," Lucia grinned, "I hope he is worthy and won't give up on pursuing you, you are a pearl among women."

"I think Ace Jackson knows how to pick the best of the best. He has a sense for these things." Guy winked at her.

Kiya covered her face, "you two are too much. My ego... my head."

Lucia laughed, "let's stop complimenting her Guy, she can't handle it."

****

On Saturday night, they sorted through the old photos. It was a pleasure to see the Rio Grande valleys in the old days. Guy had a separate box with the name Wiley on it. Kiya looked at it eagerly.

"So that is your family's photos?"

"Yes," Guy said. "My aunt Myrtle had them. I have to get some of them restored and then digitized. Lucia said she could do it."

"But it will be a big old boring project," Lucia said. "I tell you though, these pictures were so enlightening. It was interesting to see Michael 'Micky' Wiley without dreadlocks. He was a handsome dude," Lucia said. "Not that he isn't good looking now but back in the day, he was gorg."

Guy chuckled and passed the box to Kiya. "Here it is. Here is my family tree."

On the top of the stack was a black and white photo of people posing awkwardly and unsmiling. Guy had it labeled with the years beside it.

"The original Wileys," Guy said. "That's my great grandfather."

Kiya picked up a picture that was labeled the 1920s or 30s. It was of a stern-faced gentleman, he stood beside a woman with a fluffy permed style with her hand on his shoulder, three little boys, and a girl stood before them in order of height.

"What's his name?" Kiya said, looking even closer at him.

"That's Frederick Wiley," Guy said. "He is Micky's father, the lady beside him is Laurel Wiley, my great grandmother."

"He looks so much like Ace," Kiya chuckled, "Or should I say Ace looks so much like him?" Guy looked at Lucia significantly.

"I told you she would say that. That's the first thing I said when I saw these pictures. Why is my ancestor and Ace Jackson looking so much alike?"

"I swore I wouldn't say anything unless you asked…" Lucia bit her lip and worked it with her teeth.

"What?" Kiya asked impatiently.

"Micky once told Guy that he slept with Celia Jackson," Lucia said in a rush.

Kiya opened her mouth, "Say what!"

"He was her gardener, you know, and Myrtle was their housekeeper."

Kiya took up the picture again. "Woo. Good Lord. What a pickle. So this could be Ace's grandfather?"

"That's right," Guy said.

"So, who are the boys and the girl?"

"That's Michael." Guy pointed to the youngest, "And beside him is Gabriel and Uriel, then there is Myrtle, the only girl. You know, Myrtle, and you know Michael, aka Micky.

"That one," Guy pointed to Gabriel, "was my grandfather. He had two boys, Joseph and James. Joseph was my father."

"That's why you named your son Joseph," Kiya nodded, "in honor of him and Micky."

"That's right," Guy pointed at the other boy in the picture, "and that is Uriel. Whenever you hear the name Wiley in that entire region, you just quickly assume it was Uriel's children. He had a lot of kids, maybe around twenty or thirty, I think."

"There is a story about Uriel that's interesting," Lucia said, "he supposedly died and rose up again."

"How?" Kiya widened her eyes.

"He had sleeping sickness," Guy said, "and they assumed he was dead, he didn't seem to be breathing, so they wrapped him up and prepared him for burial. As you know, those days, they didn't keep bodies in refrigerators, there wasn't electricity in the valleys at that time. If you died on a Tuesday, they would bury you on Wednesday. Anyway, they were taking him to the burial spot after the church service when he woke up and started banging on the coffin."

"You lie," Kiya laughed.

"Yes," Guy grinned, "apparently, that sort of thing was not unheard of. So they let him out, got him water and food. He died at ninety-five, and when he died, they made sure that he was really gone."

Kiya opened her mouth. "I don't know what to wrap my head around. The fact that Ace Jackson could be Ace Wiley, or that they tried to bury Uriel alive?"

Guy shook his head. "I have long gotten over the Ace is a Wiley angle."

Lucia pointed to another picture. "That is Frederick Wiley's twin brother, Franklin Wiley.

"They look identical," Lucia whispered.

"Now he was a Holy Ghost filled preacher." Lucia chuckled. "They still talk about it in the neighborhood to this day. They call him Prophet Franklin. He never married. He claimed he had to be pure and without the touch of a woman's hand. They have stories about his exploits, healing people, and all of that stuff."

Lucia shook her head. "To this day, people have it that

if Prophet Franklin was alive, then so and so would not be sick."

"I heard the stories about him," Kiya said," but I am still stuck on Ace looking so much like Frederick and Franklin Wiley to even process anything else."

Guy passed her a photo of Micky again. "Remember, this was Micky back in the day, according to Lucia he was gorg."

"Yeah but still," Kiya said, "Celia Jackson is so uppity, would she sleep with her gardener no matter how hot he was?"

Lucia routed around in the stack of photos beside her and handed one to Kiya. "This is her, and this, I think, was your mother."

It was an old photo with all of them in miniskirts. Kiya looked at it closely, they all looked like they were auditioning for a girl's pop band.

"That was their high school uniform." Lucia chuckled. "You see how short the uniforms were?"

"For real?" Kiya muttered. "And that's my mom looking like a snack."

"Looking like the whole buffet." Guy laughed. "With her high hair and high heels and mini skirt, she looks like she was auditioning for the Supremes."

He took up the old photo of George in front of the shop and the one with her mother in the group shot and said, "Yup, they were an eighties couple all right."

Kiya found the picture of Frederick Wiley again. "I just can't get over this."

"We know," Lucia and Guy said together.

"I must admit that it took a little while for me too. However," Lucia said dramatically, "Guy told me that I should not jump to any conclusions about Ace's heritage."

"I don't know which other conclusions you can jump to

after seeing this picture," Kiya said. "Can I get a copy?"

"Sure." Guy nodded. "I can WhatsApp it to you."

"This is all she's going to think about all weekend," Lucia sighed. "Nothing else will make any sense. Nothing else will be entertaining, all she'll be thinking of is the prim and proper, Celia Jackson with Micky Wiley, the gardener."

"I wonder why she hates me?" Kiya asked. "I didn't know anything about this."

"Maybe she's suspicious of you because you know me. You're working for Guy, and she probably thinks you heard the rumor."

"The only rumor or the only indication I've had lately that something is amiss is Janet. She keeps saying that I should not date Ace or DJ. I should pay attention to Trey and all different manner of confusing crap. I thought she was implying that my dad was Ace and DJ's father. Both Ace and his father have laughed off what she said, I'm still not getting this."

Guy shrugged. "I'm not getting it either. So what if Ace is a Wiley. Why shouldn't you date a Wiley?"

"Maybe she thinks George is a Wiley?" Lucia asked. "George doesn't look like a Wiley."

"Their family is fascinating," Kiya said. "You know what Ace Sr. told me? He said his mother was not really married. He said that back in the days, a single pregnant nurse was not going to cut it. So his mom made up a husband and called herself Mrs. Jackson. She had two children for a phantom husband."

"The women of that time." Lucia shook her head. "They went through quite a bit, didn't they, while the men got away with everything."

"Before Lucia gets lost on a tangent," Guy winked at his wife. "I want to talk about Ace Jackson Sr.. You are saying he has no idea who his father is?" Guy furrowed his brow. "Are you serious?"

"Not a clue," Kiya said. "And strangely, it doesn't seem to bother him. If I didn't know who my father was. I would be so troubled. It could be anybody. I would be looking around in people's faces and wondering who I am." Kiya laughed. "Luckily, I don't have that problem."

Lucia snorted. "I know my father is, and to this day, he does not want to know who I am. Knowing who your biological father is, is a bit overrated, I think. Like who cares?"

"But at least you know that your father is Chilton Wray from the hardware store in Port Antonio. You know his kids, you know his family, even if he doesn't care," Kiya said. "It should suck that you have no clue, no family history. If there's anything wrong, you can't have somebody to talk to or have a way to trace it.

"Take my sister Kavina for example. She has sickle cell. So it's obvious that my mother and father were carriers of the gene. That means it is quite possible that I could be a carrier too, since both my parents are. I need to find out from my potential spouse if he is a carrier. Then I'd know that my child could possibly have sickle cell, and we prepare ourselves for our children to have the disease."

"There is that," Lucia shrugged.

"When my sister, Kavina, is feeling pain, she blames my dad for knowingly having her."

"It was just the luck of the draw," Lucia said. "You and your other sister and brother don't have it, do they?"

"No." Kiya shook her head.

"Do you want to continue looking at pictures, or do you want us to take a walk?" Guy asked. "I want to show you my latest greenhouse. It's a hothouse for roses. I didn't believe in growing anything that I can't eat, but Lucia here has convinced me otherwise."

"I would love to see it," Kiya said eagerly. "Marlene described it as glorious, more majestic than the one we have at the store. We have an order for all of the roses we have at the store, you know that. There is a bride who wants all of the roses next week, every single one."

Guy nodded. "I heard."

Kiya got up eagerly, but at the back of her mind, the thought was still ringing— Ace Jackson was a Wiley?

Chapter Fifteen

Ace agreed to meet Yara at Devon House. They would drive there separately and then have their first date. He wasn't thinking about it as some kind of romantic venture, but Yara was always funny and lighthearted to speak with, so he was anticipating a fun night.

With Yara, there was no anticipation of chemistry, no feeling that she is the one, not like it was with Kiya.

He hadn't seen Kiya for a full day, and here he was acting like he had seen her every day for all of his life. It was crazy the way he was feeling. He had relationships before. He even felt intense attraction, but he had never quite felt like this.

This is dangerous. He heard Janet's voice in his head.

This is how I felt for your mother, Ace Sr.'s voice echoed over Janet's. When you know, you know.

He drove into Devon House and parked the car and waited for Yara. It didn't take her long to show up. Yara had always been punctual. He got out of the car, and she walked toward him, grinning.

"Hey, you! So here we are. It's the beginning of the rest of our lives."

Ace laughed. "You are being funny already."

"I'm not being funny, Ace Jackson Jr," Yara said. "This is what we're going to tell our grandchildren. We knew each other for years, even though you're a slight bit older."

"Ten years," Ace said. "You used to follow us around and tell on us. When Cole, Mason, and I were playing, you used to be up front and center, like a brat."

Yara grinned. "But I'm no longer a brat, am I?"

"No, you're not," Ace said. "You are an attractive woman with a lot of potential and a lot to offer some man who will appreciate you."

"This is not starting off well," Yara growled. "Let's go again. Do you know how hard it is to find a man that's my height when I'm in heels? You fit the requirement, you're on my list, so let's go get this romance started."

Ace laughed out loud and then wiped his eyes.

"Okay, let's go get this romance started."

Yara tucked her arms through his, and they walk toward an ice cream shop.

"So I made a list," Yara said. "Of all the tall, dark, and handsome men that are in my social circle and in my radius. You made it to number two, or was it one? I don't remember. I keep crossing off people."

Ace cleared his throat. "Well Yara, that is not exactly romantic, is it? It's not something that you would want to let your date know."

"I think we should be honest and upfront with each other," Yara said. "There is no room in this relationship for dishonesty."

"So, we have moved from the first date to a relationship?"

Ace smiled. "By the time we reach the ice cream shop. We will have been married."

"Oh no, young man," Yara grinned. "You will have to ask my father for my hand in marriage."

They reached one of the shops, and it wasn't too packed. Usually, it was overflowing with locals and tourists alike.

A tall, dark guy was in front of them in the line. Yara groaned.

"What's wrong?" Ace asked.

"That's my gardener's son," Yara whispered. "He's following me."

"But we're standing behind him," Ace whispered back.

"I can bet he came here first, saw me, and decided to come in here before me."

"You are paranoid!" Ace said out loud. Yara moved behind him and tried to hide.

The guy looked behind and then said, "Hey, Yara!"

"Miss Carr," Yara said coldly. "I did not give you permission to call me Yara."

Ace raised a brow. He had never heard Yara use that snobbish voice before.

The guy just grinned, held out his hand to Ace, and introduced himself as Delano.

"Delano Dixon," he said. "I am Miss Yara Carr's, gardener's son," he said it slowly with a twinkle in his eye.

Ace smiled. "I am Ace Jackson."

"My date! And it's Dr. Ace Jackson!" Yara chipped in. Ace ignored the little byplay until after they ordered and were outside eating their ice cream.

"What's the story with you and Delano Dixon, the gardener's son?" Ace asked after a while. Yara was in deep thought. She jumped, almost upending her ice cream.

"He... er he..." Yara stuttered. "I think he's been stalking me lately."

"Why?" Ace asked.

"One evening, I was feeling sorry for myself..." Yara inhaled and then exhaled. "I went to my parents' house, but my mom wasn't there for me to tell her my problems, but they were there, a group of men, replanting some mature trees along the walkway.

"I watched them; it was fascinating to see them create a walkway of Italian Cyprus when there was none there before. Anyway, I may have taken more than a passing notice of him in the group.

"Obviously, he saw me taking notice, and when he was packing up to leave, I waved. If you didn't notice, he is tall, dark, and handsome."

Ace nodded. "As a matter of fact, I did notice that he was your type."

"I was sitting in the gazebo and staring at him, and he just came up to me and told me that he had always liked me, and he asked me if I was lonely, sitting and staring out." Yara made a face. "I said yes, I don't know why I was so honest. I guess his comment on liking me got to my head. Usually, I do not let these things get to me... And so we started chatting, way up into the night and we might have kissed. Well, he kissed me."

Ace chuckled. "So you kiss the guy, and now you are blanking him. And you think he is stalking you?"

Ace looked across to where Delano was clearly talking with another person.

"That's a girl he's with," Ace said. "He's not stalking you, Yara. Are you sure you're not the one stalking him?"

Yara made a face. "His father did say he would be here tonight."

"The plot thickens." Ace laughed. "Why isn't he on your

list? He meets your requirements."

"He's cocky full of himself and too self-assured," Yara snorted. "Besides, he's still in school. He is studying law, and did I not say he was my gardener's son? My mother would never allow a union between us."

"So, you've been considering it?" Ace smiled. "Given it a lot of thought, have you?"

"Too many thoughts," Yara sighed. "Besides, he's not on the list. Remember the list? You are on the list."

"The list needs to go," Ace said. "And your mother needs to accept her children for who they are, and their choice of mates, and give love a chance."

"You don't know my mother," Yara snorted. "I do know her," Ace said. "And I know her kind. She's my mother's friend, remember? Birds of a feather and all of that."

Yara wasn't really listening. She was turning her neck to see what Delano was doing. Ace looked around. Delano was heading toward them with the girl.

"What is he doing?" Yara murmured. "I don't want to meet his girlfriend."

"Hey guys," Delano said easily. "This is my sister, Ari. Today is her birthday, so I took her out."

"Oh," Ace could feel Yara relax beside him.

"Ari, this Dr. Ace Jackson, and Miss Yara Carr.

"Our dad works for the Carrs. Is this the same Carr?" Ari asked sweetly.

"One and the same," Delano said.

"So, is this the Yara that you have a crush on?" Ari asked not so subtly.

Delano nodded. "Yes, this is her, my future wife. But not for a couple of years. I'll have to have my own law practice, establish myself a bit, impress her mother."

"Stop it!" Yara hissed. "Why are you so bold?"

"Because I know you like me," Delano said, "and I like you too. Sorry, Ace."

Ace chuckled. "I think she likes you too, and I don't think you have to wait a couple of years. It's her you need to impress, not her mother."

"Ace!" Yara hissed. Ari was watching the byplay and finding it just as funny as Ace did.

"Thank you," Delano looked at him contemplatively. "That's good advice. I thought I would have had to warn you off."

"Yara is like a little sister," Ace said. "Even though she could have told me that she was using me tonight to make you jealous."

"That's not what happened," Yara hissed. "Ace, why are you throwing me under the bus like this?"

"Hey Ace, walk me to my car, please," Ari said. "let us leave these two star crossed lovers to figure things out?"

"Sure thing," Ace kissed Yara on her cheek. "This guy should be on the top of the list."

****

Ace reached home a little after nine. It was a Netflix and chill sort of night, but he didn't feel like watching anything.

He had started reading his father's autobiography. But he hadn't gone past the second page. He could put a dent or two in it tonight. He would call Kiya first. She answered after the first ring.

"Ace! I was just thinking about you. Is your date over already?"

Ace chuckled. "My date had a date already lined up, so I left her to it." He told her the whole story about Yara and Delano, and she laughed.

"I figured Yara wasn't really jealous of me. She's a pretty nice person," Kiya said. "She made me feel comfortable the night of your parents' anniversary party. Even though she kept warning me about you, saying you were hers, etcetera, etcetera. Now that I hear this story, I realize that there was no conviction behind that warning." Kiya cleared her throat. "So, Ace."

"Yes, Kiya." Ace said lazily.

"I am going to WhatsApp a picture to you, and then you can call me back."

Ace paused. "What?"

"Guy and Lucia were looking through some old pictures for a homecoming magazine they're going to be doing of the Rio Grande Valley, and trust me, you will want to see this picture. Okay, I'm going to send it now, and then you call me back, right back. I'm sending two."

Ace hung up and waited for the picture to be downloaded on his phone, and then he sat up.

Kiya had put the label on one, Frederick Wiley, and on another, Franklin Wiley. In the picture, Frederick Wiley was standing with his four children and his wife.

He could pick Micky out of the picture. And of course, there was Myrtle, the only girl, but what gave him pause was the fact that Franklin and Frederick Wiley looked so much like him and Deuce.

He and Deuce didn't only have the Wiley's eyes. No, no, this was showing that they had the cheekbones, the ears, the mouth. His hands were trembling a little. He felt like forwarding the picture to his mom with a caption that said, 'Sins Exposed'.

Instead, he called back Kiya. "So Franklin and Frederick were twins?" He asked. "They look just alike."

"That's right," Kiya said. There was a brief pause.

Kiya didn't know what to say, and he didn't know what to say either.

"I'm going to forward this to my mom. Ring you back tomorrow," he said.

"Ace," Kiya said reluctantly. "I am so sorry."

"It's no problem," Ace said. "I've always suspected this. I've gotten more than one insinuation about this. It is not a surprise. What is a surprise is how much I resemble Frederick and Franklin Wiley.

"It's almost spooky. Like no DNA test required, huh?" He sighed. "I'm going to call Myrtle. Really, I'll ring you tomorrow."

He forwarded the picture to his mother. He didn't bother putting a label on it. And then he rang Myrtle Wiley.

As usual, Myrtle answered the phone as if she didn't hear well. She probably had it upside down. She eventually righted it because her voice came back to normal.

"Ace, when are you coming to visit? I think I have arthritis in my fingers. I need a checkup."

"You're too used to house calls," Ace said huskily. "Are you sure you don't want to move to Kingston, up to Golden Acres with Micky? I could keep an eye on the two of you up here. There would be no need for me to take the trip to Portland every second."

Myrtle chortled. "All my nephews have offered to take me to Kingston at one time or the other. I'm not leaving home, Ace. This is my neighborhood. I grew up here, I've lived here most of my life and I'll die here."

"At least consider it," Ace said gently. "And stop talking about dying. You have at least thirty or forty years left in you."

Myrtle laughed. "If you say so, doc. So seriously, when are you coming by?"

"Next week, Monday. Easter Monday."

"I'll cook up a storm," Myrtle said.

"Don't go out of your way," Ace stressed. "Remember, you have arthritis in your fingers?"

"It only acts up sometimes," Myrtle said. "And when I rub it with Guinea hen weed in alcohol, it doesn't hurt."

"I guess Micky made that concoction, didn't he?" Ace asked.

"No, it's an old recipe," Mertle said. "Everybody knows about it."

"You country people and your recipes."

"It's better than the chemicals you keep shoveling down your throats," Myrtle said and then chuckled, "I sound like Micky."

Ace laughed dryly and then asked her what was really on his mind. "So Myrtle, tell me about your father, Frederick Wiley, and his twin brother Franklin Wiley."

"Dadda was good man," Myrtle said. "One of the best. Unfortunately, he did not believe in education. I know I've told you this before, but it's because I didn't live with my parents why I got a chance to go to high school. When you lived here as soon as you were old enough, you went on the coffee field. That was the life."

Myrtle sighed. "Take for instance, Micky. He started working at age ten. My oldest brother, Gabe, short for Gabrielle. He started at nine. Those were the days when having children meant you had ready labor for the fields."

"And Franklin Wiley, what about him?"

"Prophet Franklin was a man of God," Myrtle said with passion. "He predicted with accuracy things of the future. He healed the sick. He had the gift of healing."

"I see," Ace said slowly.

"Don't be a skeptic, Dr. Ace." Myrtle was warming up. "I

am telling you that back in the days, Prophet Franklin Wiley used to baffle doctors. They didn't like him because he was making their patients well. If he were alive now, Doctor Ace, I would be cured of my arthritis, I tell you."

Ace cleared his throat. "Really? Are you sure it wasn't the people's faith in God that made them well?"

"Oh yes," Myrtle said. "That had something to do with it, but listen, Prophet Franklin had a 100% success rate. I'm telling you; he had the gift."

"So was he married? Did he have children?" Ace asked.

"No," Myrtle said. "He was pure. He claimed that he was a first fruit of God, and he was not to defile himself with women. He wore white robes, and he had the power of healing."

Ace bit his lips, it all sounded ridiculous to him, but he was a postmodern scientist who interpreted things differently from Myrtle.

He wanted to argue, but sometimes one just needed to listen.

"I see," he said.

Myrtle went on and on about Prophet Franklin and his greatness to the point that Ace actually started dozing off.

"Hmm, Myrtle," Ace said gently. "Maybe you could tell me more when I drop by next week?"

"Oh yes," Myrtle said. "And then maybe you could explain to me why is it that I resemble your father, Frederick Wiley, and his brother Prophet Franklin."

Myrtle went silent. "How do you know how they look?" She asked after a while.

"Guy has old pictures. He's planning some magazine or the other. Kiya is staying with Lucia, and Guy and Kiya sent the pictures to me."

"You are in touch with Kiya?" Myrtle asked, alarmed.

"Is there some reason why I shouldn't be?"

"No reason," Myrtle said. "People look alike all the time, Ace." She quickly changed the subject.

"I must go now. I have something on the fire."

She hung up faster than Ace could say goodbye.

"And the plot thickens," Ace said in the darkness.

Chapter Sixteen

Kiya had to force herself out of bed after the weekend with Lucia and Guy. After the initial shock about Ace Jackson and his Wiley relatives, she had tried not to discuss it with Lucia, but it had not been far from her mind.

Today was going to be an extra-long day. She had to go into the store at seven o'clock to discuss the large order of roses they had for the wedding on Sunday. The wedding planner, Debbie Wright, was bent on clearing out the entire greenhouse, it seemed. She wanted millions of dollars of fresh flowers.

Kiya couldn't wrap her mind around it. Why spend so much money on fresh flowers? Not that she was complaining as the seller of the flowers. Why spend so much money when you could just use that money toward your new life together, or at least if you were so desirous of having flowers have it in a garden.

Anyway, people had their quirks, and it was going to add

her bottom line. It was going to be the biggest sale since she took over from Marlene. She couldn't afford to be late. She barely gulped down her tea, and she waved to Janet, who was sitting in a chair and doing some weeding.

"You're going out early today," Janet said.

"I'm going to meet with a wedding planner." Kiya grinned. "I have a large order of flowers. We might have to get some from Guy's greenhouse."

"Ah," Janet said the shocked look melting from her face. "For a minute there, I thought you were the one who was going to get married."

"Not me," Kiya said. "At least not yet. Ace hasn't asked yet."

Janet opened her mouth to protest, and Kiya giggled. "Just joking. See you later."

She headed for the car. Early morning traffic was a breeze. Probably this was the time when she needed to be out of the house.

The sun felt lovely on her skin. The city had not quite woken up yet, the hustle and bustle hadn't started.

Debbie Wright was waiting for her at the front when she got there. They went into the greenhouse together for Debbie to inspect her order.

"You don't understand what this means to me," Debbie said. "The bride is as high strung as they come. You know what her vision for this is? Flowers, lots of flowers. I don't think she has given the groom a thought."

Kiya chuckled. "That sounds like my sister. Before she got married, that was all she thought about- the wedding. I think she just wanted to be a bride."

"Are they still together?" Debbie asked. "In my experience, not thinking about the marriage spells trouble. I once had a bride who didn't know that she would have to have sex with her husband. I heard the honeymoon was a bust."

Kiya laughed. "Are you serious?"

"Yup!" Debbie said. "The husband was thinking about the physical part of the relationship, and he left all of the flowers and wedding favors and all of the music and whatever to her. She was thinking of having a fairy tale. I don't know if she was expecting them to just hold hands and walk into the sunset."

"My sister and her spouse are no longer together." Kiya frowned. "But who knows? Maybe they'll get back together soon. They are the classic case of not knowing each other."

Kiya's phone rang, and she saw that it was Kavina's number.

She answered chirpily because she knew Kavina was the type to be miserable, and she didn't want to be dragged down at the start of the day.

"Top of the morning to you, Kav," Kiya said.

"Top of the morning!" Kavina screeched. "Do you know what Dad just told me?"

She was shouting so loudly, even Debbie could hear her.

"What did Daddy tell you?" Kiya said calmly. She covered the phone and walked into the office. "Give me a second, Debbie."

"Daddy said he is not my father," Kavina yelled. "Not my father."

"Oh, wow," Kiya said, "Are you sure he said that?"

"Of course, I'm sure. And when I pressed him and asked him what he meant, he said, he is not your father, Gwen's father, or Lorenzo's father."

"Say that again!" Kiya was stunned.

"So I was blaming him for me having sickle cell, right," Kavina said, "and then Daddy stood up from the table and said, 'Kavina, I had nothing to do with your sickle cell. I'm not a carrier. Whoever your biological father is, he is a carrier.'

Then he left the table." Kavina wailed. "Just like that. This morning I woke up with a father and next thing I know I don't have one. And when I asked Daddy who my father is, he said it must be some man with a miserable gene like me."

"He's not serious," Kiya said soothingly.

"He is serious!" Kavina shouted. "He said he can't have children! He is sterile from having mumps when he was younger. What's worse, he doesn't think any of us have the same father."

Kiya gripped the hands of her office chair and sat down in it.

"He's evil!" Kavina was sobbing.

"Is Dad still there?" Kiya asked cautiously.

"No, he's not." Kavina cried. "How could he still be here, after unloading such a thing on me? He knows he has to leave and let me get on with my grieving. Don't bother calling him," Kavina hiccupped. "He left his phone."

"Where is Gwen?" Kiya asked.

"In the room, pretending that she's not hearing anything," Kavina said. "When I asked if she heard what Dad said, she said she has always known that she's not one of us, she thinks her father is a rich man somewhere and one day she was going to find him. She is not serious about this at all."

"We have the same mother, though, didn't we?" Kiya shook her head, trying to clear it.

"I think so. Have you heard otherwise?" Kavina hiccupped again. "I'm an orphan with a blood disease, and I have no family history."

She hung up the phone abruptly, and Kiya was reluctant to call her back. Kavina would eventually calm down.

Just yesterday, she was bragging to Lucia and Guy about how necessary it was to know your own father, and today she didn't know who her father was!

Kavina must have heard wrong. But why would she be crying her eyes out if she had heard wrong?

She shook off the depressing thought and went back to join Debbie.

****

Ace found his mother in his office when he went in.

"Jessica called in sick," she said bitingly, "and I'm going to be working at the front desk today."

No good morning. No pleasantries. Ace sighed.

"Why did you send me that picture, Ace Jackson?" She stressed the Ace Jackson.

"What? The one with Frederick Wiley and Franklin Wiley? Did you know they were identical twin brothers? Imagine that I have twins in my immediate family."

"They are not your family. It is pure coincidence that you look like them," Celia said. "What do I have to do to get through to you, Ace?"

"Give me your blessing for a DNA test," Ace said. "I would do it with or without your blessing anyway. This kind of evidence is just too overwhelming to be a coincidence."

Celia folded her arms and glared at him. "I will never give you permission to do something that is so against my very nature. You are implying that I was a cheat, that I stepped out on my husband with Micky Wiley. Are you crazy?"

"Mom? Your word is not enough anymore." Ace shook his head. "Could you vacate my chair, please. I have a long day ahead of me. By the way, I'll be going to Portland next Monday. I'll be getting DNA samples from Micky Wiley, and I'll be doing that DNA test. Deuce said he's interested to know the results too."

"Deuce!" Celia's eyebrows shot into her hairline. "What do you mean, Deuce? You're bringing your brother into this madness."

"He deserves to know the truth, too," Ace said.

"This is abject disrespect," Celia growled. "I have never in my life had this kind of disrespect thrown towards me."

"And I have never in my life heard somebody protest so much about something so obvious and right in front of us," Ace said. "Next Monday will be your day of reckoning. You can actually confess now, and we can move on with our lives."

"Confess to what?" Celia asked interestedly.

"That you had an affair with Micky Wiley, or you slept with him, at least twice. See you have two sons that look just like his father and his uncle. Mom, there is no getting around this."

Celia's eyes watered up. "I pray every night that you would leave this alone."

"God doesn't answer stupid prayers, Mom." Ace was getting annoyed.

"If you do this DNA test, I will never speak to you again," Celia growled and walked out of the office.

"If I don't do this DNA test," Ace called to her, "then I will be living my life in limbo. I'm tired of that. Do you know that I don't even know if Kiya and I are brother and sister?"

"It's that girl's fault," Celia threw over her shoulder. "I remember when you liked that one Lucia too, she kept implying that you were somehow a Wiley or some crap like that."

"She was wrong, now this new girl is wrong, and I just can't... I don't know what to say to you, Ace Jackson Jr."

All steam, no fire, Ace thought to himself when she flounced away, her head held high at a very awkward looking angle.

He would have to ask Kiya to do a test too. It was a conversation that he was not looking forward to having with her. Up until he saw those pictures, he had given his mother the benefit of the doubt, somewhat.

Now he was fully convinced that he was Micky Wiley's son. He needed to know if Kiya was Micky Wiley's daughter, and he needed to solve this madness so that they could all move on with their lives.

He texted Kiya to ask her if they could meet that evening. She texted back. 'Sure.'

For once, seeing Kiya would hold a certain amount of dread for him.

****

It was raining when Ace showed up at her apartment. The pleasant day had devolved into a downpour that hadn't let up since six o'clock. Kiya was nursing a vegetable broth and pacing her kitchen nervously before Ace showed up.

She hadn't managed to call her father. She had tried twice before, but he hadn't answered. And to imagine there she was sympathizing with Ace about his paternity issues when she had more than her share.

The proverb 'If you live in a glasshouse, don't throw stones' was at the forefront of her mind. There she was, condemning Celia Jackson in her head when her own mother had done the same thing. If the whole situation weren't so serious, she would have a laugh. She didn't hear the knock on the door when Ace came upstairs. The rain was pounding so hard on the roof.

He actually called her phone and said, "I'm at the door." She pulled it open. He was still in his work clothes, so obviously had just come from the office.

"Hey, you." He smiled at her weakly.

"Hey, you." Kiya raised her vegetable broth to him. "Would you like some broth?"

"No, thanks." Ace closed the door and leaned on it. "I actually want to have a serious conversation."

"Your mom confessed, and you're a Wiley?"

Ace shook his head. "My mom will never confess. This is actually about you."

"Me?" Kiya raised a brow. "What do you know?"

"Apparently, when your mother was pregnant with you, she was living with Micky Wiley," Ace said. "And there is a theory that I am really Micky Wiley's son. Ergo you and I are possibly brother and sister."

Kiya walked to the counter and slowly put down her cup. "I'm sure I'm not hearing right. We can't be brother and sister. It's just today that Kavina called me crying, Dad told her he was not our father. I haven't had the chance to speak to him yet, and now this! It is too much."

Ace sighed.

Kiya kissed her teeth. "None of this makes sense, do you know that? I have been around for twenty-six years, and I have not once suspected that I was not my father's child, and now I am hearing that I might be Micky Wiley's child, which would make me what, a Wiley?"

Ace nodded. "I guess it would."

"And you, my brother?" Kiya shook her head. "That's not even funny."

"I want to settle this," Ace said. "I'm going to Portland next week, Monday. I'm going to get a DNA sample from Micky. I'm going to test him and my brother, DJ. And if you want, I can test you too. Let's clear up all of this."

"Sarah and Abraham were brother and sister, and they got married," Kiya said. She didn't even realize she was thinking out loud.

She just knew that when she looked at Ace, she did not feel sisterly toward him, not one bit. Was that how Sarah felt when she looked at Abraham, what was she even thinking?

"Sarah and Abraham, in the Bible," Ace chuckled. "Come on, Kiya. Different cultures, vastly different situations here. If we find we are brother and sister, it would be devastating, but we would live with it, we would deal with it, and there definitely would be no marriage between us."

"What will your father say?" Kiya asked.

"I have no clue," Ace said. "I don't know what my mom has told him. I don't know what transpires between all these characters in this sick play."

Ace grabbed the door handle after giving her a last longing look. "Good night, Kiya."

"Wait. I want to come to Portland with you. I may as well visit my dad. And I don't mean Micky Wiley, I mean, George Brady."

Ace gave her a half-smile. "I wish this wasn't a joke."

Kiya inhaled. "Me too."

"I'll text you when I can come and pick you up. Good night, Kiya."

"Good night, Ace."

When he left, she locked the door and leaned on it, not having the will to move.

Chapter Seventeen

Kiya tossed and turned for most of the night. She had lurid dreams where she was marrying Ace Jackson, and the pastor declaring, 'you may now kiss your sister'.

Needless to say, she wasn't in a particularly good mood when her phone woke her at six thirty-five.

"It was about six-thirty when she had left the house yesterday, all chirpy and happy. What a difference between yesterday and today.

She answered grumpily.

"It's your old dad," George said. "I saw several missed calls from you."

Kiya's mouth was dry. She swallowed with difficulty. "Dad, Kavina called me yesterday."

"I figured she would," George said. "I was hoping she wouldn't, but knowing Kavina, she has to spread our misery everywhere, doesn't she?"

"Is any of what she said true?" Kiya asked, cutting to the

chase. She didn't want to talk about Kavina and her misery. She wanted to talk about this madness that she was suddenly encased in.

George sighed. "It's true."

It was as if her heart deflated.

Kiya inhaled raggedly. "But I don't understand."

"You know, I thought I would have gone to my grave without having this conversation," George said mournfully. "But here goes, I married Charlotte knowing that I couldn't have children.

"When she found out, she left me because she wanted children. And so she went out and got them with different people. Every time she left me, I went back for her like a stupid man," George said. "I refuse to divorce her even though she was living like a single woman. I was the one who constantly begged her to come home.

"She only came home when she was pregnant, or ran out of money, or whoever she was with wasn't financially able to take care of her. I guess I was the patsy, the one who had the means to provide for her and the children—you, your brother and sisters. The funny thing is," George said contemplatively, "Charlotte didn't even choose the men who were doing well financially. I guess Micky Wiley was the only exception because he has that big coffee farm."

Kiya gasped. "Is he my father?"

"I really don't know," George said. "The year your mother got pregnant with you, she had left Portland altogether. I heard she went to Kingston, probably Montego Bay. I don't know who your father is, really.

"I saw her in the market pregnant, heard that she was living with Micky Wiley, and I went up there, and I told her that she should come home, and she did, and she had you. And then four years later she left again, back to Micky Wiley and she died in childbirth."

Kiya sighed. "Oh, Dad. I think I had the right to know all of this."

"I didn't want you to know anything about your mother and her lifestyle," George said. "It's a tough story to tell a girl about her mother. There was a time when she went wild around the neighborhood, you know. They used to call her Charlotte-the-Harlot."

Kiya gasped. "I've never heard that before."

"And you wouldn't. Nobody dared to say it to my face," George said. "They had me as the idiot who went back for my wife when she was pregnant, but they didn't know the full story. I was guilty. I was partially guilty for how she was.

"You see, I really loved Charlotte, and I wanted her for my wife. I was a little older than her and I thought that maybe, you know, she would be happy with just me. I was wrong. I shouldn't have hidden my sterility from her. I have loved you children as if you were my own flesh and blood. And you haven't suffered because of all of this, have you?"

"No, Dad," Kiya said dutifully. She didn't want her father to feel as if she was being ungrateful, but at the same time, she found this quite appalling.

"So, it's true that Micky Wiley could be my father?"

"Biological father," George stressed, "sperm donor. It takes more than a sex act with a woman to be a father. It takes growing children; it takes being there for them. It takes waking up in the middle of the night when they're ill. It takes all of these things. It takes sending them to school. It takes financing their dreams."

"Dad," Kiya said slowly. "I am not blaming you for anything."

"You are not, but your sister Kavina is another kettle of fish," George said. "I just wanted her to stop blaming me for her blood disease. I'm not carrying any sickle cell genes. I just found it unreasonable that day in, day out she is calling me a murderer.

"Do you know that's what she's been saying, Kiya? She's calling me a murderer because she has sickle cell and she's going to die. I snapped. I could not handle it one more day, I tell you. One more rant from Kav, and I'll go crazy. Right now, she's crying. She cried throughout the night, asking me 'so who is my dad?'

"Do you know who her father is?" Kiya asked.

"I think I know," George said. "I'm not sure, but it could be Milo Jenkins she resembles his family, with the hazel, cat eyes."

"Milo Jenkins!" Kiya gasped. "Are you sure? The guy that does the mountain tours and has the fake cowboy accent?"

"Yes," George said. "Your mother lived with him in his hut, and she got into a fight with one of his ladies. She came back home, bloodied and bruised and pregnant with Kavina."

"Good heavens." Kiya whistled.

"I told Kavina that," George said, "and since I told her she's been crying and wailing. I can't stand it, Kiya. I can't stand it. When I tell her to control herself, she's saying how I'm going to send her to Milo Jenkins' hut. The man doesn't even live in a hut anymore."

Kiya tried not to laugh. It wasn't funny, but she could imagine Kavina saying just that.

"And who is Gwen's father?" Kiya asked.

"I heard that Gwen's father was a Spanish tourist who had his yacht here. He docked at the marina for a weekend."

"That explains the grey eyes and the silky hair," Kiya murmured. "Oh my. And Lorenzo?"

"His father is Toots Carter. He died a long time ago. I knew Toots quite well, and he knew me, and he knew he was sleeping with my wife. He used to tell me about it all the time when I saw him in the market. He mocked me with it. I never said a word."

"I'm coming over with Ace Jackson, next Monday," Kiya said faintly. This was too much information for her to process. "I'll come and look for you. I miss you, Dad."

"I miss you too, Kiya. I wish you were here, my only reasonable child," George sighed. "I must apologize for not letting you know all of this before. I didn't realize that it would mean so much to you.

"The truth is, I've never considered any of you children, any less than mine. I had you with me when your babies. Your mother always left the children, and I didn't mind taking care of you one bit."

"Thanks, Dad," Kiya choked up. "I'm going to have to get up and get ready for work."

"Okay, hun." George hung up. Kiya stared in the ceiling. It was confirmed.

Kiya Wiley. She repeated in our head, it didn't quite sound right.

Kiya Brady sounded better. Kiya Brady Jackson, except there would never be a Kiya Jackson. Ace Sr. didn't even have the name legitimately, and Ace Jr. was not a Jackson. He was probably also a Wiley.

Good heavens, the twists in this tale.

She had to move at record speed, it was getting late. She jumped up out of bed, not even bothering to spread it. She would do that when she came back. She had a shower and put on her clothes. When she was on her way out, she realized that Janet's door was open.

Celia Jackson was standing on the step, a murderous look on her in her eyes.

"What have you been telling my son?" She asked.

Janet hobbled behind her. "Leave the girl alone, Celia!"

"Hi Kiya," Janet said chirpily. "I hear the puss is out of the bag. Your father called me last night."

Kiya nodded jerkily. "And then I called Celia, here to gloat that I was right, and she showed up at my doorstep, acting so rude when I think she should be treating you with the deference and respect as one who is sister to her sons."

"Shut up, Janet, before I step on your foot and break the rest of your toes," Celia growled. "You have been a busybody too long, all up in my business, saying things that aren't true, giving people impressions that aren't right."

"She was loose-living," Janet said over Celia's shoulder, "cheated on her good, good husband, with the gardener, Micky Wiley—who was a spouter of nonsense.

"He used to say things like education is out to get us and all different kinds of stuff. That's who she had an affair with. No offense to your biological father, Kiya, but he has one nail hanging loose in his head."

"There was nothing wrong with Micky." Celia couldn't restrain herself from defending Micky Wiley, "and I don't appreciate my business being blasted out on the front step of your home."

"I just came here to tell Kiya Brady to stop filling my son's head with crap."

Kiya stood stunned. She didn't know what to say. Luckily for her, Janet was the one who was gleefully having the conversation with Celia.

"If you hadn't stepped out of your marriage to Ace Sr., who has never been unfaithful to you, then you wouldn't be here, standing like a martyr, wondering if anybody is buying what you're selling. You are guilty," Janet said. "Guilty of loving the gardener, and now it's coming home to roost."

She gave a good approximation of a witch's cackle.

Celia winced.

Kiya left them at the front. She was late already. She had no time for this.

Chapter Eighteen

Ace was on his way through the front door on Easter Monday when his father drove up.

"Where are you going?" Ace Sr. asked. "I thought we could hang together today. I have more pages of my autobiography to add to the manuscript you have. And I found some juicy tidbits about my mother in Tobias' journal.

"Florence sent down a box of Tobias' things. Things that she thinks I would be interested in. And I was going through it this morning and voila. I found something that was usable. Something that explains a bit about my heritage."

"That's very interesting, Dad." Ace felt guilty. He had been deliberately avoiding his father for the last couple of days, always feigning busyness because he didn't want to tell him what he suspected, and what he was up to.

Ace Sr. frowned. "Too busy for a juicy tidbit. Why are you acting suspiciously?"

"I am not!" Ace said indignantly.

"You sound like when you were a boy, and you were caught doing something that wasn't quite right." Ace Sr. frowned. "Are you planning to elope with Kiya and rob me of my speech to you at your reception?"

"Elope with Kiya?" Ace frowned. "No Dad. That is far from what I am planning. I'm planning to go to Portland, and she's coming along."

"Ah, Portland," Ace Sr. said wistfully. "If I wouldn't be a third wheel, I would come along. We could go to my old childhood hot spots, even though I'm sure they're vastly different now."

"There are some things that never change, especially in the Rio Grande where change comes slowly." Ace looked at his father strangely. "You never want to go to Portland, you avoided it like the plague. What's happening to you?"

"Maybe it's the notebook I just read that I found in Tobias' things. He was a poet, you know. He waxed poetic about the green lushness of the place, the blue-green waters of the Rio Grande, the semi-precious stones that were used to collect, the succulent sweetness of the fresh fish that we used to catch from the river."

Ace folded his arms and looked at his father. "So Tobias' journal brought back memories?"

"Oh, yes." Ace Sr. nodded. "Some of the things I quite forgot. You know, he lived a kind of Huckleberry Finn kind of childhood; he had the river, which was a stone's throw from his backyard and his own boat. He had many stories to tell about the river and the surrounding hills too, he made some ridiculous observations in his adventurous journeys.

"And now here I am thinking that Tobias' journal is probably more entertaining than my autobiography.

"He makes Portland come alive. The Blue-Green Mountains, the clear sea, the mangoes, the plums, the friendliness of the people.

"He spoke quite a bit of all the people in the neighborhood too." Ace Sr. sighed. "I had quite forgotten about Miss Perkins."

"I remember Miss. Perkins," Ace said, torn between hearing what his father had to say and knowing he had to go.

"No, you remember her daughter. The original Miss Perkins was in Tobias' time. She used to do the best, and I mean this, the best fried dumplings ever. I don't know what that lady put in them, but the outside was nice and crispy, and the inside was so tender and soft. Not to mention her saltfish fritters.

"You haven't lived until you had one of that lady's greasy salt fish fritters. She used to sell them in a paper bag.

"You know those brown paper bags? Whenever she'd put six of the fritters in there, you'd see the grease rising at the side, and that was so good with some lemonade."

"Dad!" Ace cleared his throat and looked at his watch. "As much as I'd like to hear you reminisce about Portland, I really promised to pick up Kiya."

Ace Sr. smiled hazily. "I know. Let me not keep you. May you have a great trip. Maybe you and I, DJ and Trey, can go at another time together and explored the place."

That was completely out of character for his father.

Ace frowned at him. "Are you sure you're okay?"

"I am sure," Ace Sr. said. "My love for Portland is like a relationship. Something happens, and you fall out of love with the person, but then you hear somebody else talking about her, and then you remember how beautiful she was, and all of the good experiences you used to have. That is how I am now with Portland, thanks to Tobias, I remember my love.

"The memories are making me nostalgic. It was a good

neighborhood, Ace. They were good people."

Ace had his hand on the car door handle, but his father was still speaking.

"You know, my childhood yard?" Ace Sr. asked.

"No," Ace turned around. "I remember when we lived in Portland, we lived at that big house with the hill and gardens."

I never had the chance to show you boys the real Portland, the Portland of my youth," Ace Sr. said. "And I'm so sorry about that."

"That's okay, Dad," Ace said. "We survived without a tour."

"I wasn't around much, was I? I wasn't the type of father that I wanted to be. I was just chasing the dollar. I wanted to be wealthy enough so that I could move out, because I remember what it was like not having much, materially. I didn't realize that I was doing it at the expense of you boys having the kind of childhood that you should have."

"Dad, where is all of this coming from?"

"Regret," Ace Sr. said. "Anyway, you are going to take a picture for me. You're going to take a picture of the house where I grew up. Well, I'm not even sure if there's still a house there, I still want to see what's become of it."

"It's beside George's shop. The place to the right of it. There were two houses in the yard. At the front was this Georgian style house that was made of stone. That was where my grandparents lived.

"At the back of that, my mom lived in more modest accommodations. And to the back of that was the Rio Grande. We used to go down the hill and catch fish for dinner. There was a jetty at the back, where my grandfather kept his boat…"

"Tell you what, Dad," Ace said. "I'll take a picture. I don't know if the houses are still there, but I'll take a picture, and

I'll WhatsApp it to you. Is that okay?"

"That's fine." Ace Sr. smiled. "Run along, and tell the lovely Kiya, hello." Ace nodded.

When he went to pick up Kiya, he was shocked to see her standing at the gate with boxes and boxes of foodstuff, he assumed.

"I didn't know you were planning to stock George's shop." Ace laughed.

Kiya smiled. "He called me on Thursday, before the holidays started, and said I should go shopping for buns. He told me what he wanted, and here they are. I wanted to tell you to expect luggage, but you weren't answering your phone."

"It was a hectic week," Ace said, trying to avoid the accusation that he heard in her voice.

"It's okay. I figured you were trying to avoid me. I would try to avoid me too. I have been grumpy all week. My staff has been calling me Jekyll and Hyde."

"So what have you been up to?" she asked after he loaded all of the boxes and bags into the car. There was no space left on the backseat, when she was done.

"I've been up to this and that," Ace said. "Trying to keep busy and away from my potential sister."

Kiya shook her head. "This is crazy, you know that."

"But alas, it is our lot in life," Ace said. "I think this is the best time to meet, and I think it is better to clear this up now rather than later."

"I agree," Kiya said, "but it doesn't make it any easier, does it? Our mothers were something else. I've been trying to think charitable thoughts about mine, but it's not working. I spoke to your aunt Janet this week.

"She said everybody knew my mother slept around and they shunned her even when she was at church. Nobody wanted her near their husbands, and no mother wanted her near her sons. I probably would turn up my nose at her as well," Kiya said. "It is shocking that was who she was."

"In the five stages of grief for her reputation, you are now at anger," Ace shook his head. "She was who she was. I have nothing bad to say. I don't think Janet, my mother, or anybody else should be judging her.

"Maybe at the end, she made it right with her maker, who knows. He who is without sin cast the first stone."

Kiya looked at him. "That's magnanimous of you."

"We all have our little quirks," Ace said. "Not that we should be comfortable with having them, but we shouldn't be pointing fingers and ridiculing others. We should do some self-examination. I said as much to my mother who was trying to denigrate yours. I wouldn't be taking this trip if there wasn't something questionable about her actions too."

"Ah." Kiya nodded.

"By the way," Ace said, changing the subject. "Did you know that my grandparents used to live beside your father's place?"

"No, really?" Kiya said, "that was probably a long, long time ago."

"My father wants me to take a picture of it. He said back in the days there were two houses on that piece of property. It was on a slope that led to the river below."

"I know it. That is the Witter's place now. They built steps that go down to a jetty and have a boat tied up behind there. There are still two houses on the lot," Kiya said, "but the front house is modernized. It's a big white edifice. I think they are doing Airbnb there now. The backhouse is a guest house, a two-bedroom guest house kind of thing, and they have a pool. Your father wouldn't recognize it now. It was a nice piece of property. Why did he sell it?"

"He wasn't the one that sold it. His uncle Tobias sold the place when his parents died. Nobody was living there at the time; my grandmother, his sister had left Portland by that time and was living with him in the States."

"Nurse Jackson." Kiya smiled. "She was a popular midwife here. They had two midwives in this area. Nurse Jackson and Nurse Tulie.

"Nurse Jackson never lost a baby under her watch. I was kind of shocked when your father said that she didn't have a husband. I wonder who her lover was?" Kiya asked.

Ace chuckled. "Well, you could go investigating the mystery of Nurse Jackson's phantom lover, my grandfather."

"I guess there are worse things than not knowing who your grandfather was," Kiya said.

"Yes. Like not knowing who your father is. That's much worse. But you'll soon know." Ace patted her leg and then dragged back his hands quickly.

Kiya smiled. "If we turn out to be brother and sister, you are not going to touch me any at all?"

"Nope, not even with a pole." Ace shook his head. "And we will never speak about the fact that we were attracted to each other. And we will not be alone in a room, nor will we meet face to face on a regular basis."

"It's that bad, huh?" Kiya grinned.

"Why do I think you like this a little bit too much," Ace said. "Are you a pervert, Kiya?"

"No," Kiya said, "just really happy that you feel that way, which probably makes me a pervert," she said under her breath.

"It's different when you know," Ace said. "I am pretty sure they're married couples in this world who blindly go through life not knowing that they're blood relatives."

"I don't want to be Micky Wiley's daughter," Kiya said.

"And I don't want you to be his son. What do you even know about Micky Wiley, anyway?"

"He's an interesting character," Ace said. "He has strong opinions on everything from gardening to the state of the world. And he's not afraid to let you know that he doesn't want any modern ideas to brainwash him."

"Yup. I remember Micky Wiley's drunken rants at Daddy's shop. I used to think he was almost as bad as Milo Jenkins. Milo Jenkins, the village jester, is my sister Kavina's father. Charlotte was not really discriminatory, wasn't she?"

"How are your sisters taking this?" Ace asked. "This was like a bombshell going off in your family."

"According to Dad, Gwen is indifferent. She always knew she wasn't the same as us, because of the grey eyes, I guess," Kiya said. "But Kavina is not taking it well, especially after Daddy suggested that Milo Jenkins was her father. It is making her hysterical. She's keeping to herself, much to Greg's chagrin. He's her boyfriend, the only one who knows how to calm her down, so this is not good."

"She is fortunate she has someone like that in her life." Ace said, "she shouldn't be shutting him out."

"That's true," Kiya said. "He knows Kavina. He loves her unconditionally. I think he is very near in getting her to say yes to his marriage proposal, I guess when she finally decides to give him the time of day, it will be an end to an era in our household.

"My brother is gone. Gwen is married, Kavina will be married, and I'm gone to Kingston. My dad will be an empty nester."

"He will probably throw parties every night." Ace grinned. "Oh wait, he already does that."

"Your aunt Janet might come back home," Kiya said slyly.

"Janet would be too much for George. After all, he's

been through with his first wife, I think that he would want somebody more on a mellow, less dramatic scale in his golden years."

"Or maybe that's the type he likes," Kiya said. "Women full of drama and intrigue."

****

When they entered the Rio Grande Valley area, Ace inhaled deeply. It was a different air in the deep countryside. He always loved coming to this area. He understood why Guy Wiley couldn't stay away. It was as if a small burden was lifted when you entered the lush green valleys.

"So I'll drop you off at your dad's, and then I'll take a quick picture and head up to Micky's place," Ace said. "It will take a while. Myrtle likes to talk."

"I know," Kiya nodded. "Just give me a call. I'll be ready when you get down."

Ace dropped her off, greeted George and his ever-present patrons who were playing dominoes at the front. There were four Domino tables set up. Obviously, the tournament had grown. When Ace had lived in the valleys, it had been only two tables with men standing around waiting their turn to play.

George helped Ace take the boxes out of the car. George was looking a tad shaky, not the robust man that Ace remembered. He had more gray hairs, and he had lost a ton of weight.

"You changed your diet, George." Ace said to him when they said their hellos.

"Yes, Doc." George nodded. "That and the fact that Kavina is nagging me into slimness,"

Ace chuckled.

"My dad asked me to take a picture of next door. I'm just

going to walk over."

"You won't be able to see much," George said. "They have up high fences now. It's quite fancy over there these days. Not that I'm complaining. When visitors come, they come to my shop."

Ace nodded. This stretch of road was more developed than he had realized and in such a short period of time. Or maybe he hadn't really looked closely at the place before.

He had a tendency to drive through what they thought of as the town area. He got a peek through the gates and took a picture. His father will be very disappointed. It is not what he was imagining, he was sure.

Chapter Nineteen

Ace headed towards Micky's Hill, or that is what he was calling it in his head. From the bottom of the hill to the top was newly terraced. Before, it was wild, but now it had retaining walls made of stone and white blooming shrubs blanketing the hill.

Ace was sure the plants were Micky's doing, and Guy had conned him into beautifying the place because Micky hated change.

There were even streetlights leading from the bottom to the top. One mile from the house and leading up to the Hill was smoothly asphalted.

Ace had to congratulate Guy in his head. He had really dragged the Micky into the twenty-first century.

When Ace drove up to the house, he could see that Guy had worked his magic up here as well.

It was a two-story edifice that had a brilliant view of the Rio Grande the river below. It was also freshly painted and neat. As usual, Micky was in his garden at the top. He looked nothing like an 80-year-old man.

His locks were floor-length, but he kept it up in a turban.

His dark skin hardly showed any wrinkles, and of course, there were the eyes, the Wiley eyes, the familiar-looking eyes that he saw in the mirror every day.

Micky had a way of smiling with his eyes and his mouth. He lit up when Ace stepped out of the car.

He was weeding around a plant. He brushed off his hand and got up.

"Doc, what's up, man?"

"Nothing's up, Micky." Ace grinned. I came to check up on you".

"I am blessed, Micky said. "I have so many people checking up on me, but I must tell you, Doc. I have no aches or pains. No coughs or sniffles. You know my sarsaparilla works, man. And I take my guinea hen religiously every night. And if I feel a little sniffle coming on, I take my rum and lime."

Ace chuckled. "I get the point, Micky."

"Your medications are of the devil, man." Micky said. "But I don't hold it against you, Doctor. You, I personally like. Your medicine I think is poison to the body. We should all take God's medicine, the sun, the rain, the food from the ground, no salt, no sugar, sometimes abstain from food and sometimes go raw."

"Goodness, Micky," Myrtle said from the veranda. "Ace just arrived. Couldn't you allow him to breathe before you start on your medicine is of the devil crap."

Micky laughed. "I don't talk to him often enough."

"Because you refuse to use the telephone," Myrtle said.

"That thing will rot your brain," Micky said. "Mark my words. They'll soon find rot in the brain from the telephone."

"Micky, it's a good thing that Ace is used to you."

Ace smiled at Myrtle. "How are you, Myrtle?"

"I am good," Myrtle said. "It's good to see you. Come on in. I have been baking and cooking all day in anticipation of your coming. Can I tell you how excited I was? Come spend some time with somebody who is not anti-establishment, anti-education, anti-religion, anti-everything."

"You insult me, Myrtle," Micky said. "I am not anti-education. I'm just anti the education they tell us that we have to learn in the institutions they set up to brainwash the masses."

Myrtle rolled her eyes. "Come along, Ace."

Ace reluctantly left Micky. He always liked to hear his opinion on everything. They were unusual, but sometimes Micky made sense.

He wasn't only thinking that because there was a very high chance that Micky was his father. He had always warmed up to Micky's unusual take on life.

"Come through on the back patio," Myrtle called as they headed to the house. As usual, the place was clean, and the hardwood floors were glistening. Inside was repainted a cream-white color, which made the place look bigger, and there was a TV set in the corner.

Ace gasped. "You have a TV in the house?"

Myrtle laughed. "Yes, but it was quite an ordeal to get Micky to agree to it. And when it's on, he says he does not want to walk near it, because, as he says, the rays from the television will rot his lungs or his kidney or some other place in his body.

"He has accused Guy and Lucia of trying to carry the evil rays up here to rot us out. But somebody has to carry Micky kicking and screaming into this century."

"Is he really okay, health-wise?" Ace asked. "I know he has a thing about telling me, his doctor, whether he is okay or not."

"He's fine," Myrtle said. "He stopped drinking everything but his own homemade beer. He still smokes his marijuana though," Myrtle said. "That you cannot stop him from doing. Last week he went to a Nyabinghi session and said in the midst of chanting, he got a vision. He said he saw Prophet Franklin in a vision asking him to forgive him."

"Is that so?" Ace sat at a table on the patio and looked out at the beautiful view. He could see the river winding around the hills in the distance.

"I can't get over how pretty this place is," Ace said. "It's like you guys are at the perfect spot. You won't be affected by flooding, and it is constantly breezy here."

Myrtle sat across from him. "You aren't hungry, Ace? Because I have a whole lot of food."

"Not ravenously hungry or anything," Ace said. "But I made sure not to eat before I came here because I knew you would have a spread."

"Good boy." Myrtle grinned. "You know, I used to be your nanny for the first five years of your life."

Ace nodded. "Yes, Myrtle, you tell me this every time you see me."

"I was there the day you were born," Myrtle said. "I helped with the delivery. Seeing you now makes me feel so old. How is your mom?"

"She's good, I guess," Ace said. "She's not talking to me at the moment."

"Why?" Myrtle asked.

"Because I'm going to do a DNA test. I want to test to see if Micky is my father."

"Ah," Myrtle nodded.

"And I see that doesn't shock you."

"Not at all," Myrtle said. "You do have a look of the Wiley's about you. I said it the day you were born, but she begged me not to say anything to anyone."

"How long were they together?" Ace asked.

"He was their gardener for three years," Myrtle said. "And they used to be in the house a lot, and they didn't have any house plants if you know what I mean."

Ace made a groaning sound.

"The truth is, while I was there," Myrtle said. "I noticed that they acted a bit too familiar with each other, and I used to talk to Micky about it, but I think after Deuce was born and he looked so much like a Wiley, your father packed up and left here so fast.

"Or should I say your mother's husband. Since we don't really know if he is your father, do we?"

Ace grunted.

You know it has always shocked me that they stayed together for all these years. Now that's love," Myrtle said. "I've seen couples leave each other for less."

"Yes," Ace said. "They're quite dedicated to each other. Myrtle, tell me about Charlotte Brady."

"Charlotte Brady." Myrtle shook her head. "That girl went through a lot. I mean, for such a pretty girl, you would have expected a different life, but Charlotte did not value herself one bit.

"She used to live here for a while, you know. I always used to say, while watching pageants on TV these days and I'm seeing the girls that that are winning Miss Universe and Miss World and all of these things, and I'm saying if Charlotte Brady had entered, she would have to win, hands down.

"She was a beautiful girl, but she had such low self-esteem. She kept having children for all these different men, sleeping around here, there, and everywhere."

Ace sighed. "This is not good news, Myrtle."

"Why?" Myrtle asked.

"Because I like Kiya, well, it might be a little more than mere liking her. Do you know if Kiya is Micky's daughter?"

"I can't say," Myrtle sighed. "When Charlotte first came here, I suspect she was already pregnant. She wasn't showing, mind you, but I guessed she was pregnant. She had morning sickness and was trying to pass it off as an upset stomach. I think she liked living here for a while, and so she wanted Micky to take care of her. When I confronted her about it, she confessed that she was pregnant, but she wasn't sure who she was pregnant for. It could be Micky; it could be anybody."

Ace inhaled and then exhaled raggedly. "Wooh, that's not particularly good news for me, is it?"

"No," Myrtle shook her head.

Ace sighed. "I need a swab from Micky's cheek. Do you think he will allow it?"

Myrtle nodded. "Funny enough, I think he will."

"Why?"

"As I was saying to you before, he went to Nyabinghi, and he had a dream or a vision or something."

"At the risk of sounding ignorant," Ace said, "What is a Nyabinghi?"

"It's a Rastafarian gathering, kind of like church, they chant scripture, beat drums, smoke their chalice, and speak of unity. It's kind of like church but with a different flavor," Myrtle grinned, "It's as close to church as Micky is ever going to get.

"Apparently, Micky smoked a wisdom chalice, and he saw Prophet Franklin in the vision. He knew it was Prophet Franklin because he was in a white robe."

"And Prophet Franklin was your father's twin brother?" Ace said. He was now well versed on the Wiley family tree by now.

"That's right." Myrtle nodded. "Prophet Franklin... We weren't allowed to call him Uncle Franklin because he was set apart, chosen by God. He always wore white robes. He walked through the district with a bell around his waist. He prophesied. He baptized people, and he healed."

Ace cleared his throat. "Pardon my skepticism, Myrtle, but did he really do any of those things? Was he really effective?"

"He was," Myrtle nodded. "I'm telling you. We had a sleeping sickness disease in this area. It was everywhere in Jamaica, but I'm telling you, in this particular area, only five or six persons got it. If prophet Franklin prayed over a house, they didn't get it. And anybody who had the disease would wake up if he touched them."

Ace snorted. "I am sorry, Myrtle. I'm still not convinced. I'm a twenty-first-century man, and all of these things just seem odd."

"I know, but back in the days before there was this period of enlightenment and over the counter medication, there was Prophet Franklin," Myrtle said. "So anyway. Franklin got the gift when he was young. My father told me a story about his mother getting a cut on the foot and coming home. Apparently, Franklin touched it, and when she woke up the next morning, it was healed."

Ace was trying not to show his incredulity.

"And so the legend of Franklin was born. Yes," Myrtle nodded. "We all knew this as children. Prophet Franklin was the chosen one, pure and holy and undefiled. He never had any children, he just lived to be a prophet and then died on the very day that he said he would. He is buried in the family plot."

Ace cleared his throat. "So when Micky was high on marijuana at the Nyabinghi session, the prophet told him what?"

"Prophet Franklin told him to do as Ace says," Myrtle said. "As clear as that, and then he told him I am sorry."

"Well, I guess I should be saying thanks to Prophet Franklin," Ace said, not really believing a word about Micky and his vision.

"I guess you should." Myrtle got up now that her storytelling was done. "I have a spread you will not believe. I have roasted breadfruit, ackee and saltfish, and I don't mean the saltfish that you get from the supermarket. I salted this fish myself. I cured it in my cooking hut."

"Ah," Ace nodded.

"That's just for starters," Myrtle headed out. "And I baked so many puddings today in my outdoor oven. I want you to take back some for me, Ace. Could you do that? Shawn, Aisha, Sheryl, Sandrene, and the others love my puddings. I baked one for every Wiley household, including yours." She winked at him.

Ace did not have the energy to protest that his wasn't a Wiley household, but she could be right. He could be a Wiley.

Micky joined them on the veranda shortly after Myrtle served the food, and they chatted. Micky was a fountain of information about everyone in the neighborhood.

"One would think," Ace said to Micky, "that you wouldn't know anything since you live all the way up here, and away from everyone."

"But I go to the hub, man," Micky said.

"George's shop," Myrtle murmured. "Where he's the reigning Domino King. And when men are drinking and playing dominoes, they talk about everything. They spill secrets and make up some," Myrtle snorted. "I can't stand down there. George has a TV in a shop and Micky has no problems with the waves from that TV. George plays music there, and Micky has no problems with the beat from the speakers."

Micky smiled angelically. "She's just jealous, man. She wants me to stay up here with her and keep her company when big things are going on in this world and in this neighborhood."

After they finished eating and Myrtle cleared the table.

Ace said to Micky. "I need to get a sample from you, just a swab with a cotton tip from the side of your cheek."

"Nah man," Micky said. "There is nothing wrong with me, Doc."

"I know," Ace said, "but Prophet Franklin told you that you should do as I say, didn't he?"

Micky looked alarmed. "This is it? This is why he wanted me to say, yes?"

Ace would use anything at his disposal to get that sample from Micky, including going along with this ridiculous story.

"I think so," Ace nodded.

"So why did he say sorry, though? And why do you want my cheek sample?"

"I'm going to do a DNA test once and for all," Ace said, to check that we are not related, or that we are."

Micky nodded. "Very well, I don't know much about these things, you know, the scientific things."

"I know," Ace said, looking at him fondly. Micky was quite an interesting man.

"But if Prophet Franklin says I should do it, then who am I to question the Prophet. You can't question the Prophet," Micky said.

"No," Ace said, "I'm going to go and get my things."

Chapter Twenty

The Tuesday after Portland was not particularly an easy day to face his father. Ace was going to need his DNA, and it wasn't a conversation he was looking forward to having. His mother was filling in for Jessica again, and she glared at him when he stepped into the office.

"Had a good day at the Flower Show, Mom?" Ace asked pleasantly.

"I only speak to my children when they're obedient. Disobedience does not endear me to you, Ace."

Ace laughed. "And there I was thinking that parents had unconditional love for their children."

"I do love you," Celia said, "but I don't like you right now."

"Why, because I want the truth?" Ace asked incredulously.

Celia turned her back to him, and Ace shook his head and walked into the passageway to his office. He saw his father's car outside. So he knew he was there already. Usually, the day after holiday was very busy for the practice, so he had to get this done quickly.

When he checked the electronic appointment system, he saw that his father was going to have an appointment in the next ten minutes. He would have to make this snappy.

He grabbed the testing kit, walked back out into the hallway, past his mother, who looked at the cup in his hand. She knew what it was, and she was not pleased.

"Ace, I beg you. Why are you bringing this back up?"

"Because I have to," Ace said.

His father's office was in the opposite hallway. The door was opened. Ace Sr. looked up with a smile.

"Hey Ace. I saw the picture that you sent. I really need to take a trip over there if that is what the old place is looking like. And when did George add a jerk center?"

Ace smiled. "Well, Kiya said he built it in the past three years. He has a gathering out there that could rival any Boston Jerk Festival at certain times of the week. He sent a jerk fish with Kiya. I'm going to have some later."

"Jerk fish on a wood fire," Ace Sr. smacked his lips. "Good golly, I can almost taste it now."

"He has a chef working there," Ace said, "He looks like a pro wrestler, but he's as gentle as a teddy bear and has the skills of a master chef or so Kiya tells me."

He placed the cup gently on Ace Sr.'s desk. "Dad, I know you have an appointment in nine minutes or so. I am going to do a DNA test, and I need your sample." He had decided that not beating around the bush was the best way to do this.

His father nodded briskly.

"Okay." Ace Sr. did the test himself, placed the cotton swab back in the bottle, labeled it, and handed it to Ace solemnly.

"You do know that even if this says that you are not biologically mine, you are still my son."

Ace nodded. "I know Dad, but I just want to know. I can't

believe that you have never done a test. The lab is just next door. In all our growing up years, you have never felt like you should?"

"No," Ace Sr. said. "I love your mother, and you are a part of her. Are you going to test DJ too?"

Ace nodded.

"It hadn't escaped my notice that you and DJ closely resemble each other." His father said.

"Is that why Trey has always been your favorite?" Ace asked.

"Ha," Ace Sr. said. "I have no favorites. For a little while, Trey seemed as if he was going off-kilter, and he needed more attention than you and Deuce. Trey was a stubborn, and rebellious child, and teenager and I'm frankly shocked that he's actually a functioning adult now. You may not remember, you're seven years older than him after all, but when you were in college, your mother and I really struggled with Trey.

"What you interpret as favoritism was us panicking. The three of you have different qualities that I admire. You are the responsible one. I've never worried about you, Ace. Well, until lately, when I realized that you're going to be hitting the Big Four O, and there is no woman in sight. "You know a father wonders about being a grandfather. We can't help it. It's annoying, but we just can't help it."

Ace inhaled raggedly and took up the container. "I love you, Dad."

"I love you too, Ace," Ace Sr. said. "I always have, and I always will."

His mother's eyes were red when he passed her at the front desk. She didn't make eye contact with him, and Ace felt a tad bit guilty, but why should he feel guilty?

A child always had a right to know, but yet his mother's

downcast expression really haunted him that day.

It haunted him when he went to the lab and handed the vials to Tracy. She was the lab assistant who usually did stuff for him.

"Dr. Ace, we are swamped, and we are behind," Tracy said, "way behind. When do you want these? Is it life or death?"

"These are DNA tests," Ace said. "And this is personal."

"Oh," Tracy rounded her mouth. "Is this in vitro for an unborn baby?"

"No," Ace said, "Nothing like that. I'm just testing a couple adults from my family."

"Okay," Tracy said. "Well, I guess it isn't urgent."

"As soon as possible would be nice," Ace said.

"ASAP will be Friday." Tracy looked at her calendar. "You can collect it Friday evening."

"Thank you," Ace walked through the door, feeling apprehensive. His world was about to be turned upside down.

He thought of Micky, and then his dad. He realized that he didn't want that kind of change in his life.

Knowing would change things. He almost turned back to take his sample out of the lot. He didn't take that action because it was always better to know.

Not only because of curiosity, but he wasn't sure, one way or the other if he was Kiya's brother. There was that angle.

Kiya texted him near lunchtime: *'my place or yours, for the jerk fish?'*

Ace didn't have much time for lunch. So he texted back, *'my place.'*

It was only when Kiya walked into the small dining room that he remembered that his mother was working there today. Based on the mood that his mother was in; he was sure there would be some form of a clash. To his surprise, there wasn't.

The dining area was relatively small. It had two tables and

eight chairs. It had a fridge, a coffee maker, and a microwave. His mother came in for some tea. She put on the kettle, greeted Kiya pleasantly, made her tea and left.

"Wow, she's actually acting nice," Kiya said. "I'm not used to her being so polite and non-grumpy."

"Maybe she's tired of fighting," Ace said, "and none of this is your fault, so her reaction toward you was quite unnecessary. With me, on the other hand, I am getting the cold shoulder for unleashing this scourge on her family."

Kiya chuckled. "How did your father take it when you said you are going to test him?"

"He took it all in stride," Ace said, "He's acting way more mature about this than my mom."

"I am sure it's not easy being the one at fault," Kiya mused. "And then when you think you have buried the past and you have moved on, far away from that past, here it comes. That's why some women never tell, you know. At least she was honest with your dad from the beginning, wasn't she?"

"I don't know about the beginning," Ace said, "but when he found out he left Portland, and I don't think he has ever gone back."

"So when will the results be out?" Kiya looked down on her fish. "I'm feeling a little nervous about it, to be honest. It feels like my final chemistry exam. I loathed the subject, and I was on tenterhooks for every exam, but I went into the finals trembling in fear."

"I am feeling some apprehension too," Ace said. "It will be ready by Friday evening. Three days is a long, long time."

Kiya made a face. "Am I going to see you at choir practice this Wednesday night? Solomon sent the song. Did you see it? It is for family day."

"Family day is next month," Ace said.

"Yes, but this is an unfamiliar song," Kiya said. "Solomon

said he wrote it. The first line says, 'you are a brother to me.' When I saw it, I was like, is this a sign, Lord?

"The second line says, 'And you are my sister, together, we will minister because we're a family.'

"I thought about it, and I don't want to be your family, at least not by blood," Kiya said.

Ace smiled at her. He covered her hand with his and squeeze her fingers. "I understand exactly what you're feeling, Kiya, but I'm also feeling a wee bit optimistic. Remember, Myrtle, said your mother might have already been pregnant?"

"I will not feel optimistic until all of this is over, and all the results are in." Kiya laced her fingers with his and squeeze him back.

And he found that he didn't want to let her go.

****

Celia Jackson slipped into her husband's office when there was a lull. Rarely did they have a full waiting room because the appointment system was efficient, and Ace Sr. did not have any more patients for the day.

"I can't believe he went and did it." She slumped in the chair across from her husband.

"I can't believe it took him so long," Ace Sr. said. "Now that is a boy who is obedient to his mother. You had him under your thumb for years, guilting him into not checking, and then he met Kiya."

Celia made a face. "I can't even maintain not liking that girl. She's quite a nice girl, isn't she?"

"Yes, she is," Ace Sr. said. "He is keen on her. I have never seen him like this before, you know, so certain, and so different."

"I know," Celia said downcast.

"What's in the darkness will come to light," Ace Sr. said. "What was hidden will be found. What was... "

"Norman, can you spare me the clichés?" Celia said agitatedly. "I'm so nervous I don't know if I'll ever sleep until he gets these results. This will change everything."

Ace Sr. swung in his chair. "Or it will change nothing. You know, I have a patient who, for years, thought she had cancer. For twenty-two years, she lived her life with an assumption that she had cancer. She never came in and did a test. She was afraid of visiting the doctor. She didn't want to confirm a thing. She just wanted to bury her head in the sand.

"Her theory was, if she started to get sick, then she would know that her cancer was worse, she would prepare to die. And you know what happened, Celia?"

"What?" Celia asked. Here she was agitated, and there was Ace Sr. giving her a story about a woman who thought she had cancer.

"She didn't have cancer," Ace Sr. said. "She spent years and years worrying about a sickness she never had. This is a life lesson, listen carefully, wife."

Celia chuckled. She liked it when he called her wife playfully, especially at this pivotal moment in her life.

"A wise man once said, it is always better to know."

"But you never wanted to know," Celia said.

"I did," Ace Sr. leaned back in his chair. "But I assessed the pain point, and I said, is this something I can live with? Can I live with these children, not knowing if they're mine or not? When I considered it, I realized that I could, and I did.

"As the years went by, it didn't bother me one bit. I decided to stay with you, regardless. So what would it matter?"

"Maybe you are right," Celia said. "I've spent too many years atoning for this sin, and maybe it's really better to know."

Chapter Twenty-One

Deuce called Ace on Wednesday. "Hey man, you have the results yet?"

"Nope, Ace said. "I won't have them until Friday."

"Now that sucks," said Deuce. "I would love to know if I'm my father's son before that."

"You're too funny," Ace said.

"I had a little downtime," Deuce said, "and I had time to think about it, and I must confess that I'm feeling a little bit nervous."

"I understand what you are saying," Ace said. "I think mom and dad are nervous too. But of course, nobody will admit this."

"Are we still meeting at your house to practice for church?" Deuce asked.

"Sure," Ace said. "I won't open the results until you get here."

"Cool," Deuce said. "At least we'll give you each other

some moral support, huh?" And then he paused. "Hey Ace, have you ever wondered? Suppose we don't have the same father."

"And yet we look alike?" Ace asked.

"Well, there is that," Deuce chuckled. "Unless our mother was with more than one Wiley person. Have you ever thought about that?"

"No," Ace said, "and I wouldn't imply that to Mom. She's already up in arms about me doing this. I am so happy that Jessica came back to work today because I couldn't stand her silent glares or her long-suffering, 'Ace, why did you do this to me?' You know, she hasn't said a word about this to me since I sent in the swabs to the lab?"

Deuce grumbled. "Maybe she doesn't want to add to your burdens."

"Anyway," Ace said. "I'll catch you on Friday, okay?"

"Okay," Deuce said.

Friday evening couldn't come soon enough for Ace. He called Tracy twice, and twice Tracy assured him that it would be ready, and she would call him when it was.

"Don't call us, Dr. Ace. We'll call you," she chuckled.

It wasn't a joke. Ace moved extremely slow on Friday. His father jovially greeted him with, "So it's DNA day!"

"Ha." Ace wished he could be as casual. "When are you going to get the results this morning or in the evening?" Ace Sr. asked.

"This evening," Ace said. "Your mom is having Janet over this evening. They're planning some decorating business for the church; they were picked to do it together, or else Celia wouldn't do it, she is on the outs with Janet at the moment."

"Okay," Ace said. "I was thinking of coming over, but maybe I shouldn't. DJ and Trey will be at my house for practice."

Ace Sr. shook his head, "No, you should come over. Whatever the results, I'm sure that Janet especially will be very much interested to hear. Whatever the results are, it should be all out in the open," Ace Sr. nodded. "Have a good day, son."

"As if I could have a good day." Ace murmured under his breath.

Kiya also called him, quite anxious to hear the results.

"Want to come to my house later?" Ace said. "You can open your results with me."

"I'll do it," Kiya said, "definitely because the suspense is driving me crazy."

"I am going to send you detailed directions to my home," Ace said, "or better yet. I should come and pick you up. There is no way you'll find it on your own."

"Thank you," Kiya said in relief. "I am still a newbie at driving around town. I get nervous driving from Janet's to here, and it's such a clear route."

"Well, pick you up at six. Is that okay?"

"Sure," Kiya said.

He went to the lab with laden legs. Tracy handed him the letters with a smile.

What was she so happy about? Ace thought sourly.

There was change in these unassuming looking envelopes.

He drove to Kiya's and pushed in a soothing gospel jazz CD to listen to. He was trying to take his mind off the envelopes in the back.

He had placed them in the backseat as if they were passengers.

Kiya was waiting for him when he drove up. She got into the car and looked in the back seat and then at him fearfully. "Are those the results?"

"Yup." Ace said.

"Are you sure you want me along on such a momentous occasion for your family?"

"There's no one else I'd rather have along for this ride," Ace said.

Kiya smiled. "Well then, let's go hear the good or bad news."

They hardly spoke on the way to his house. Their minds were weighed down with weighty matters.

Kiya commented on the house when they got there. "this is not a single person's house."

"I inherited it from my uncle, Tobias," Ace said. "I put it through extensive renovations, and you're right. It's not a single person's house."

He scooped the envelopes out of the car, unbuttoned the two top buttons on his shirt, and inhaled.

They went inside to the open-plan living room, and Ace place the envelope on the center table. He and Kiya sat down on settees opposite to each other and stared at the envelopes.

"Are we waiting for your brothers?" Kiya asked.

"Do you want us to?"

"You can wait for them," Kiya said. "I want to read mine." Ace handed her an envelope that had her name on it. She opened it without any fanfare.

"Kiya L. Brady," she looked on the numbers, "Michael Wiley, 0.0000% chance of being related, Ace Jackson Jr., 0.0000% chance of being related." Kiya whooped and did a little dance. "I'm not a Wiley, and I'm not a Brady, but I'm still happy." Kiya laughed. "I am not related to you."

"So Myrtle called it right," Ace said.

Kiya nodded. "Yes she did."

She went to sit beside Ace and held his hand. "You are not my brother."

Ace turned to her and kissed her thoroughly, only the

knock on the front door breaking them apart.

"That kiss was pent up," Ace murmured in her ear.

Kiya giggled. "Maybe you should answer the door."

Ace whispered. "I can't walk. I get so weak in the knees."

"What makes you think I can walk?" Kiya said breathlessly. "Besides, I don't want to answer your door and shock your brothers."

"Oh, they won't be shocked," Ace said.

He eventually got up after a knock sounded at the door again. It was his mother and father and Janet. Behind them were DJ and Trey.

"It's like a mini family reunion," Ace Sr. announce, walking past him.

Ace stepped aside. "Did you all coordinate coming here at the same time?"

"Nope. Just drove up and saw them at the door," Deuce said. "Have you opened the results yet?"

"No. Kiya opened hers. She is not a Wiley," Ace said.

He closed the door after Trey walked through. "I can't believe you guys have drama going on, and I was not aware of all of this. Why am I being left out of the family loop? DJ had to clue me in this evening."

"Sorry," Ace shrugged.

Everybody was seated in the living room, except his mother. She was in the kitchen. It was an open plan concept, so he could clearly see her in their pacing with a glass of water in her hand.

"Come and sit down, dear," Ace Sr. said. "It's not the end of the world, you know?"

Celia shook her head. "When is Ace going to get on with this?"

Ace picked up the envelope and inhaled deeply.

"Ace Jackson Jr., 99.999% related to Ace Jackson Sr."

His mother slammed the glass down on the countertop and came around to the family room.

She was clearly surprised.

"I am my father's son," Ace said in astonishment.

"Read mine," Deuce demanded. "I can't believe this. Am I the one who is not Daddy's son?"

Ace tore through the envelope for DJ results. It was the same 99.99% related to Ace Jackson Sr.

"Maybe Celia went over to the lab and messed with the result," Janet suggested. "There is no way you are Ace Jackson Sr.'s sons. You look too much like the Wileys for this to be possible. Besides, Celia was sleeping with that gardener for years."

"Actually, I was not, Janet," Celia said coldly. "Yes, I had a few encounters with Micky Wiley near the time when Ace was conceived, and then I broke it off. And then I had a one-night stand with him after that near the time when DJ was conceived. It wasn't like I was having some years-long affair."

"But it was still an affair," Janet murmured. "Don't try to whitewash this."

"And you have rubbed it in year in year out," Celia said. "But now you know, my sons belong to my husband. Argument done. Stop now, Janet. It's over! It was the toughest thing to tell my husband, and now the elephant in the room is dealt with."

Celia turned to Ace. "I must apologize, son. I was quite wrong for assuming that you should not know who your father is. Especially because you have met the girl that you love."

She turned to Kiya. "I'm so sorry, Kiya, for my earlier attitude. I hope that we can be friends one day."

Kiya nodded, but she was still confused. "So why is it that

Ace looks so much like Micky's father, Frederick Wiley?"

Ace Sr. cleared his throat. "I can help you with that question."

Everybody turned to him.

"I was telling Ace that while reading through my uncle Tobias' journal, I found out that a regular visitor to our home was the Prophet Franklin.

"We lived on the river side; my mother occupied a small house at the back of my grandparents' property. Franklin would enter from the river side. He would moor his boat to the back and walk up to the house, usually under cover of darkness. No one could see him coming and going from there."

Janet gasped. "The Prophet Franklin? You are crazy. The Prophet Franklin was pure and untouched by women, and he healed people."

"According to Uncle Tobias' journal," Ace Sr. said. "The Prophet Franklin was a nightly visitor to the house. He couldn't believe it himself when he saw him. At first, he naively thought that he was doing some healing at the house, but then he realized that it was a regular occurrence, and his sister was not sick.

"It was only after my brother Jacob was born, that he put two and two together. He asked his sister if she was involved with the Prophet, and she never said yes or no."

"The Prophet Franklin was dipping his toes in the water, so to speak?" Janet laughed. "I thought I had heard it all. Are you sure it was Franklin and not Frederick, Micky Wiley's father?"

"Tobias said he was sure it was the prophet, one night he even frightened him and he took off running, he tripped and cut his arm in the dark, the next day Prophet Franklin had a cut on his arm and was going around and telling people he wrestled with the devil the night before."

Everyone laughed.

"Your children outed the prophet and your mother with their lies." Janet chortled.

Ace looked at his father and smiled. "So that's why you wanted to go to Portland. You found your answers, the single nurse, and the single prophet. I guess you are going to have to rewrite a couple pages of your autobiography."

****

They spoke way into the night. The brothers didn't get a chance to practice. It was one o'clock before Ace dropped Kiya and Janet home. He helped Janet to the door and then turned to Kiya, leaning in for a kiss.

"Say, Kiya Brady," Ace whispered. "Would you like me to walk you to your door?"

Kiya nodded. "Yes sir."

"Our courtship begins now," Ace said. "I don't know if you realize that."

"I figured," Kiya smiled. "Since you and I are not brother and sister."

Ace walked her to her door and then stood at the doorway. "You do realize that from the first moment our eyes locked, there was something special between us, don't you?"

"I do realize," Kiya said, "it was instant, our connection."

"And you do realize that after almost losing you, because I thought we had blood ties, I don't want to lose you again?"

Kiya nodded. "I don't want to lose you either, Ace."

He pulled to him and kissed her. "I love you, Kiya."

"I love you, Ace."

The End

Here is an excerpt from Deuce
(The Jacksons Book 2)

Some people are meant to be together and I now know that you and I are destined to be....

Deuce read the first part of the message incredulously.

I was wrong and stupid to let us go. Throwing away fourteen years of memories was foolish. Please can we meet?

Deuce read the message again and fought the urge to reply with a terse, *no*. He wouldn't entertain her; he would not respond at all.

Kelsey was writing as if they had just broken up, and she didn't have three years and a marriage to another man under her belt.

So she was back. Good for her. And she was single and ready to mingle and as usual, he was her pit stop on the journey to finding herself.

This is how it has had always been for them. They would break up, usually because of Kelsey's desire to see other people and he would hope for her to come to her senses and they would pick up where they left off when she claimed that she did.

When they had broken up the last time, Kelsey had sent him a similar text except, it had read more along the lines of: *some people are meant to be together and I now feel within with my heart that it's not you and me. Dale Julius is the man that God has ordained for me, I hope you understand.*

Now all of a sudden, she wanted to give their relationship a try again. He felt resentful, but he also had a perversely happy feeling. She was no longer with Dale Julius, the other DJ.

He looked at the message again and wonder if he should respond. *How's Dale, your husband? Well, ex-husband, the one that God was supposed to have found for you.*

However, that would be showing some sort of emotion and he did not want to reveal any of himself to Kelsey Baker Julius—freshly divorced from his best friend in med school.

He knew the marriage would not have worked between Kelsey and Dale. They had two vastly different personalities.

Dale was a quiet unassuming fellow, and Kelsey was an extreme extrovert who couldn't sit still, who was always up for an adventure. Dale was not equipped to put up with Kelsey's dramatics. Only someone who loved her would put up with her mercurial temperament. Someone who knew her from they were kids and loved her despite all of her quirks.

He was that person, had been that person, he corrected in his head, but he didn't know if he still felt that way anymore. What he felt for Kelsey now was more along the lines of apathy and indifference, but she was not in his vicinity at the moment and her bid to win him back had just started.

He had been in this position before with her, where he thought he had well and truly moved on, but she wheedled her way back in his life.

He got in his car, feeling thankful that for next couple of months, and the foreseeable future, he would be working regular hours. His stint at the children's hospital was over and he was back to his practice where he set his own hours.

His phone pinged and he saw that another message had come in. He picked it up before starting his car. He wondered if it was a new text from Kelsey. He had no doubt that the message that he received this morning was just the start of her campaign to woo him back.

In the past he fell for her, 'sorry I didn't mean it' story line every time without fail.

He wouldn't be surprised if she sent him a picture of her face with a tear in one eye. He wished there was some way to inoculate himself from her.

When he checked the message it wasn't a picture from Kelsey, it was a message from his text pal, Dani.

She had taken her clients on a tour the day before.

He imagined that she was a tour guide of some sort, but he did not ask.

It was a picture of the sunset. A beautiful swirl of pink and red swaths surrounded the dying sun as it sunk into the sea.

He texted her back. *Where is this?*

Her reply: *Crimson Hills, Trelawny. It's a beautiful place. We picked up a passenger, still trying to figure out what to do with her.*

Interesting, Deuce texted back. *Who is this passenger?*

A woman running from something. Dani texted back. *She won't give us any information, had a cut on her forehead. We have a doctor looking her over. Are you a doctor, DJ?*

Deuce grinned. For all they're going back and forth in the past year and a half, they were both careful not to give away any details about each other.

Asking him if he was a doctor was a blatant violation of their unspoken rule— don't get too personal.

He didn't know if he was ready to meet her or if he even wanted to. His time with Kelsey had hit him hard and he was still wary of getting too close to anyone.

Technically, he knew that not all women were like Kelsey. He knew that it was not all drama all the time.

He contemplated Dani's question. *Are you a doctor, DJ?*

Maybe it was time they changed the rules and found out more about each other. Maybe she was the one who would break his Kelsey spell.

His fingers hovered over the phone for a while as he contemplated this next step, he typed in, *yes.*

And then, he typed, *what do you do?*

The die had been cast; he was moving forward...

OTHER BOOKS BY BRENDA BARRETT

The Jacksons Series

Ace (Book 1)- It was an open secret in his family that Dr. Ace Jackson Jr. resembled his parent's former gardener Micky Wiley and not his father Ace Jackson Sr. Ace was fine with not finding out one way or the other if he was really a Wiley until he met Kiya Brady, the rumored love child of Micky Wiley…

Deuce (Book 2)- Dr. Deuce Jackson had loved one woman all his life, Kelsey Channer. She left him, breaking his heart in the process. But now she was back. He was going to have to choose, Kelsey the woman that had broken his heart once or Dani, the woman he had never met in person who had his heart now.

Trey (Book 3)- When Dr Trey Jackson found out that his emergency patient was a stripper from Jaded Nightclub. He realized two things quickly, this was not just any stripper, this was Kenya Kyle, his one-time love, the woman who had almost ruined the trajectory of his life and second he never stopped having feelings for her…

Quade (Book 4)- Quade Jackson's housekeeper was a mystery, she called herself Grace, when that was obviously not her name, and she was hiding something. After two years of skirting around their obvious attraction to each other, Quade was determined to find out exactly what she was hiding.

Pryce Sisters Series

Baby For A Pryce (Book 1)- Giselle Pryce had a bright future, two scholarships from Ivy League schools and a track career that was going somewhere, when she discovered she was pregnant. She had several decisions to make.

Right Pryce Wrong Time (Book 2)- Tiana got her high school teacher James fired for inappropriate conduct because of her jealousy. When she meets him again as an adult in a different situation, she has no idea how to act.

Yours, For A Pryce (Book 3)- Toddy Pryce offers his favorite sister Elsa to his young political rival Mason Magnus in exchange to not run against him in the next elections.

Wiley Brothers Series

Between Brothers (Book 0)- The beginning of the Wiley brothers saga, Joseph Wiley's unconventional family life may prove to be fatal to some members of the family.

For Pete's Sake (Book 1)- Preston has a run in with a child named Pete who claims that he is the grandson of their former housekeeper Pamela Stone.

Crossing Jordan (Book 2)- Jordan is miffed when Shawn takes her new fiancé to Jamaica and insists that he be man of honor at their wedding.

Fire and Walter (Book 3)- Walter's past came rushing to greet him shortly after his appointment as church elder. The new pastor was his childhood molestor, his wife was his ex from college and her cousin was the girl who got away. Walter had a lot of decisions to make.

The Perfect Guy (Book 4) - After a patient five years waiting for Lucia, Guy had his work cut out for him to prove himself worthy of her affections. He had played the part of poor farmer for too long and now he had competition in the form of the handsome doctor Ace Jackson.

The Patience of A Saint (Book 5)- Something was wrong with Saint's wife Sandrene. It didn't take a genius to see that she was changed beyond all recognition. Saint had to get to the bottom of it, before it was too late for them to salvage anything from the relationship.

A Case of Love (Book 6)- After a concert, Case is offered a girl to buy. Her fate was in his hands. He could keep her or leave her to the mercy of her evil family.

Resetter Series

Never Too Late (Book 1)- Addi finds out she is a resetter and goes back to the summer of 92 to change her family's lives.

Never Say Never (Book 2)- Skyler's handsome college lecturer, who happens to be her neighbor, has a 't' in his palms. Should she tell him the significance of it. If she does, would he believe her?

Now or Never (Book 3)- Ten years later Addi and Randy meet again at Randy's engagement party. Why is it that the chemistry between them was still so potent? Can they ever have a future together? Would Randy choose her this time around?

Almost Never (Book 4)- Tech genius Joshua Porter had all but given up on love. He then meets Portia, an inmate at the female penitentiary and his life takes a turn for the adventurous.

The Scarlett Family Series

Scarlett Baby (Book 1)- When the head of the Scarlett family died, Yuri had to return home to Treasure Beach for the funeral. What he didn't count on was seeing Marla, his childhood sweetheart and his best friend's wife. And when emotions overwhelm them and a few months later Marla is pregnant, Yuri wants the impossible: his best friend's wife and the baby they made together...

Scarlett Sinner (Book 2)- Pastor Troy Scarlett realizes the hard way that some sins are bound to be revealed, like the child that he had out of wedlock with his wife's mortal enemy from college. His wife Chelsea was not happy with the status quo. She was not taking care of the son of the woman she had so despised from college. And she could not get over the deep betrayal that she felt from her husband's indiscretion.

Scarlett Secret (Book 3)- Terri Scarlett had a soft spot for her friend, Lola. She was funny and sweet and they looked remarkably alike. But when Lola's Arab prince demands his bride, Terri foolishly exchange places with her friend and they meet up on a world of trouble.

Scarlett Love (Book 4)- Slater always looked forward

to delivering packages to the law firm where he could get a glimpse of the stunning female lawyer, Amoy Gardener. Unfortunately, for Slater a woman like Amoy would not take him seriously, especially when she found out that he could not read!

Scarlett Promise (Book 5)- Driven by desperation Lisa Barclay decides to make some extra money by prostituting herself after being kicked out in the streets. Her first customer turns out to be a popular government senator and then to her horror he dies...

Scarlett Bride (Book 6)- When Oliver Scarlett's missionary work in the Congo region was coming to an end, he had a decision to make, marry Ashaki Azanga and save her from being the fourth wife to the chief of the village or leave her to her fate and get on with his life...

Scarlett Heart (Book 7)- After receiving a heart transplant shy librarian Noah Scarlett started to take on character traits that were unlike him and he kept dreaming of a girl named Cassandra Green...

Rebound Series

On The Rebound- For Better or Worse, Brandon vowed to stay with Ashley, but when worse got too much he moved out and met Nadine. For the first time in years he felt happy, but then Ashley remembered her wedding vows...

On The Rebound 2- Ashley reinvented herself and was now a first lady in a country church in Primrose Hill, but her obsessed ex friend Regina showed up and started digging into the lives of the saints at church. Somebody didn't like Regina's digging. Someone had secrets that were shocking enough to kill for...

Magnolia Sisters

Dear Mystery Guy (Book 1)- Della Gold details her life in a journal dedicated to a mystery guy. But when fascination turns into obsession she finds herself wanting to learn even more about him but in her pursuit of the mystery guy she begins to learn more about herself...

Bad Girl Blues (Book 2)- Brigid Manderson wanted to go to med school but for the time being she was an escort working for her mother, an ex-prostitute. When her latest customer offers her the opportunity of a lifetime would she take it? Or would she choose the harder path and uncertain love with a Christian guy?

Her Mistaken Dreams (Book 3)- Caitlin Denvers dream guy had serious issues. He has a dead wife in his past and he was the main suspect in her murder. Did he really do it? Or did Caitlin for the first time have a mistaken dream?

Just Like Yesterday (Book 4)- Hazel Brown lost six months of memory including the summer that she conceived her son, and had no idea who his father could be. Now that she had the means to fight to get him back from the Deckers, she finds out that the handsome Curtis Decker is willing to share her son with her after all.

New Song Series

Going Solo (Book 1)- Carson Bell, had a lovely voice, a heart of gold, and was no slouch in the looks department. So why did Alice abandon him and their daughter? What did she want after ten years of silence?

Duet on Fire (Book 2)- Ian and Ruby had problems trying to conceive a child. If that wasn't enough, her ex-lover the current pastor of their church wants her back...

Tangled Chords (Book 3)- Xavier Bell, the poor, ugly duckling has made it rich and his looks have been incredibly improved too. Farrah Knight, hotel heiress had cruelly rejected him in the past but now she needed help. Could Xavier forgive and forget?

Broken Harmony(Book 4)- Aaron Lee, wanted the top job in his family company but he had a moral clause to consider just when Alka, his married ex-girlfriend walks back into his life.

A Past Refrain (Book 5)- Jayce had issues with forgetting Haley Greenwald even though he had a new woman in his life. Will he ever be able to shake his love for Haley?

Perfect Melody (Book 6)- Logan Moore had the perfect wife, Melody but his secretary Sabrina was hell bent on breaking up the family. Sabrina wanted Logan whatever the cost and she had a secret about Melody, that could shatter Melody's image to everyone.

The Bancroft Family Series

Homely Girl (Book 0) - April and Taj were opposites in so many ways. He was the cute, athletic boy that everybody wanted to be friends with. She was the overweight, shy, and withdrawn girl. Do April and Taj have a love that can last a lifetime? Or will time and separate paths rip them apart?

Saving Face (Book 1) - Mount Faith University drama begins with a dead president and several suspects including the president in waiting Ryan Bancroft.

Tattered Tiara (Book 2) - Micah Bancroft is targeted by femme fatale Deidra Durkheim. There are also several rape cases to be solved.

Private Dancer (Book 3) Adrian Bancroft was gutted when he returned to Jamaica and found out that his first and only love Cathy Taylor was a stripper and was literally owned by the menacing drug lord, Nanjo Jones.

Goodbye Lonely (Book 4) - Kylie Bancroft was shy and had to resort to going to confidence classes. How could she win the love of Gareth Beecher, her faculty adviser, a man with a jealous ex-wife in his past and a current mystery surrounding a hand found in his garden?

Practice Run (Book 5) - Marcus Bancroft had many reasons to avoid Mount Faith but Deidra Durkheim was not one of them. Unfortunately, on one of his visits he was the victim of a deliberate hit and run.

Sense of Rumor (Book 6) - Arnella Bancroft was the wild, passionate Bancroft, the creative loner who didn't mind living dangerously; but when a terrible thing happened to her at her friend Tracy's party, it changed her. She found that courting rumors can be devastating and that only the truth could set her free.

A Younger Man (Book 7)- Pastor Vanley Bancroft loved Anita Parkinson despite their fifteen-year age gap, but Anita had a secret, one that she could not reveal to Vanley. To tell him would change his feelings toward her, or force him to give up the ministry that he loved so much.

Just To See Her (Book 8)- Jessica Bancroft had the opportunity to meet her fantasy guy Khaled, he was finally coming to Mount Faith but she had feelings for Clay Reid, a guy who had all the qualities she was looking for. Who would she choose and what about the weird fascination Khaled had for Clay?

The Three Rivers Series

Private Sins (Book 1)- Kelly, the first lady at Three Rivers Church was pregnant for the first elder of her church. Could she keep the secret from her husband and pretend that all was well?

Loving Mr. Wright (Book 2)- Erica saw one last opportunity to ditch her single life when Caleb Wright appeared in her town. He was perfect for her, but what was he hiding?

Unholy Matrimony (Book 3) - Phoebe had a problem, she was poor and unhappy. Her solution to marry a rich man was derailed along the way with her feelings for Charles Black, the poor guy next door.

If It Ain't Broke (Book 4)- Chris Donahue wanted a place

in his child's life. Pinky Black just wanted his love. She also wanted him to forget his obsession with Kelly and love her. That shouldn't be so hard? Should it?

Contemporary Romance/Drama

After The End--Torn between two lovers. Colleen married her high school sweetheart, Isaiah, hoping that they would live happily ever after but life intruded and Isaiah disappeared at sea. She found work with the rich and handsome, Enrique Lopez, as a housekeeper and realized that she couldn't keep him at arms length...

Love Triangle: Three Sides To The Story- George, the husband, Marie, the wife and Karen-the mistress. They all get to tell their side of the story.

The Preacher And The Prostitute - Prostitution and the clergy don't mix. Tell that to ex-prostitute, Maribel, who finds herself in love with the Pastor at her church. Can an ex-prostitute and a pastor have a future together?

New Beginnings - Inner city girl Geneva was offered an opportunity of a lifetime when she found out that her 'real' father was a very wealthy man. Her decision to live up-town meant that she had to leave Froggie, her 'ghetto don,' behind. She also found herself battling with her stepmother and battling her emotions for Justin, a suave up-towner.

Full Circle- After graduating from university, Diana wanted to return to Jamaica to find her siblings. What she didn't foresee was that she would meet Robert Cassidy and that both their pasts would be intertwined, and that disturbing questions would pop up about their parentage, just when they were getting close.

Historical Fiction/Romance

The Empty Hammock- Workaholic, Ana Mendez, fell asleep in a hammock and woke up in the year 1494. It was the time of the Tainos, a time when life seemed simpler, but Ana knew that all of that was about to change.

The Pull Of Freedom- Even in bondage the people, freshly arrived from Africa, considered themselves free. Led by Nanny and Cudjoe the slaves escaped the Simmonds' plantation and went in different directions to forge their destiny in the new country called Jamaica.

Jamaican Comedy (Material contains Jamaican dialect)

Di Taxi Ride And Other Stories- Di Taxi Ride and Other Stories is a collection of twelve witty and fast paced short stories. Each story tells of a unique slice of Jamaican life.

Made in the USA
Monee, IL
21 February 2021

61057436R00118